KV-512-321

Concannon

Trouble looms as homesteaders move onto rangeland owned by Steven English. The settlers request assistance from the army, and so US Marshal Zachary Concannon, who lost both an eye and an arm in the war, is deputed to restore law and order.

When Steven's only child, Clare, is kidnapped, Zachary rescues her and marries her in a union of convenience. But their marriage doesn't work, and Zachary travels to Canada where he finds the former slaves who had been his childhood friends, and who had been sold like cattle by his father.

Returning to the US, Zachary becomes marshal of an oil boomtown. Here, he hopes, he can realize another ambition, and meet someone faster with a gun than himself. And let the devil take the consequences.

Concannon

A.C. WAUGH

A Black Horse Western

ROBERT HALE · LONDON

WES
1403146

Typeset by
Derek Doyle & Associates, Liverpool.
Printed and bound in Great Britain by
Antony Rowe Limited, Wiltshire.

Chapter One

He knelt by the door of the cabin, his left shoulder against the cold grey stones that he and his wife had so lovingly put into place. He wondered how many times he'd crouched at the barricades, gun in hand. He'd been with Rosecrans at Chickamauga, in July of '63, when the Confederates under Braxton Bragg had pushed them back and pinned them down in Chattanooga. For a month they'd held out until General Grant himself had finally defeated Bragg. Then he'd been with Sherman in Georgia. Now, here he was in Montana Territory. This was their home, their future, and no one would take their home from them. He heard a whimper from behind him.

'Keep under the table, Mary,' he said to his wife.

'Come out, sodbuster!' someone yelled from the darkness.

'Send that good-lookin' wife of yours out!' someone else yelled, and people laughed.

'Hey, sodbuster,' the first voice called, 'see that glow? I think your barn's on fire.' More laughing.

The man leapt up and peered out the peep-hole in the window shutters. He could see flames leaping from their partly constructed barn. 'Bastards!' he screamed.

Three horsemen rode into view; he couldn't see their faces with the glow of the fire behind them. 'We have to come back, sodbuster, we'll burn the house down with you in it.' With this, they spurred their horses into a gallop and rode away.

The man, his wife and children, watched their barn slowly turn to ashes. 'They won't drive us out, will they, Pa?' their ten-year-old son asked.

'No, Pete, no one will drive us out, will they, Mary?'

His wife squeezed his hand, 'No, Charlie.'

The barman in the Mountain View saloon in Deer Creek, Montana Territory, was polishing glasses, preparing for the evening rush. He turned when he heard footsteps. A tall man stood at the bar, about 6'2" the barman guessed. He wore a Union Cavalry cloak, a battered black hat, and an eye-patch over his right eye. A scar, vivid against his tanned skin, ran from his hatline, down under the eye-patch, across the corner of his mouth, and finished at the bottom of his chin.

The man dumped his saddle-bags and rifle on the bar and asked for a whiskey. 'Weather always like this?' he asked.

'No, gets cold in the winter,' the barman replied cheerily.

'Oh great,' the man replied, and drained his drink, then shuddered. 'Another,' he said. 'Have one yourself.'

'Thanks, Mister. . . ?'

'Concannon. Zachary Concannon.'

'Joe Malone,' the barman responded. 'Here on business?'

'Sort of. Can I get a room and a meal?'

'Sure can.' He produced the register and the man signed his name. He ordered a steak with all the trimmings. 'I'll be by the fire,' he said. 'See if I can thaw out a bit.' He threw his saddle-bags over his shoulder and picked up his rifle. Dumping his gear on a table and pushing it near to the fire, he gathered his cloak around him and sat. As he watched, Joe Malone smiled to himself. It was only late summer and already it was bitterly cold. It was going to be a long, cold winter. He took Zachary Concannon a whiskey.

People began to drift in and Joe went about his business. Two farmers whom he had seen earlier headed for the blacksmith's, came in, and there was some good-natured banter about crops and stock. The atmosphere changed when three cowboys from Top Hat arrived. The farmers were instantly on the defensive, the cowboys on the prod. Joe Malone didn't like it, having come from farming stock himself, but what could he do? Farmers settling on what had been Top Hat land, had caused friction and quite a few fights. It was commonly known that Steven English, owner of Top Hat, was determined to move the farmers on.

'Come on, Lou, leave them alone,' Joe said to Lou Talbot, one of the Top Hat hands.

'Leave them be,' Joe heard someone else say. He turned, it was Zachary Concannon who had spoken.

Lou Talbot and his friends moved to where the man in the cloak sat. 'You say something, One Eye?' Lou challenged.

'Yes, I said leave those men alone.'

'And just why would I do that?'

'Perhaps because they aren't doing any harm. Perhaps because you're annoying me. Or perhaps it's just because you're a loudmouthed bastard who likes intimidating people who can't stand up to you.'

Lou Talbot went for his gun, but before it was halfway out, Zachary Concannon thrust his hand from under his cloak, holding a .45. 'Go ahead, mister,' he said, 'show everyone here you're stupid as well as loud.'

No one moved. The three men stared at the gun the seated man held. 'Put your guns on the table,' he told them. They did so.

'Now sit.' Grudgingly they got chairs and sat. Zachary slid his gun back under his cloak. 'Now isn't this nicer? All of us sitting by the fire. Joe, a bottle and three more glasses please,' Zachary Concannon asked. His hand came out from under the cloak and he poured himself a glass of whiskey. He nodded to the bottle. 'Help yourself,' he said.

'Drop dead,' Lou Talbot replied.

A waitress brought his meal. 'Thank you,' Zachary said. 'Put it in front of my friend, please.' She did and hurried off.

'I won't drink with you, I sure as hell won't eat with you,' Lou said spitefully.

Zachary Concannon gave him a cold smile. 'I don't want you to eat it, mister, I want you to cut it up for me. I can't hold a gun on you desperadoes and cut it myself.'

'You're joking, right?' Lou Talbot asked.

'Am I laughing? No. Now come on, nice bite-sized chunks.' When Lou had finished cutting, Zachary reached out with his left hand, took his plate and proceeded to eat. 'Marvellous,' he said when he had finished, 'How about coffee and pie?' he asked the waitress. 'You boys like coffee and pie?' he asked. They didn't. After finishing, Zachary sat back. 'Now that's better. You boys can go now. Try working on your social skills; you're not all that good as dinner companions.'

The cowboys stood and retrieved their guns. Louis Talbot looked at Zachary Concannon sitting completely at ease. Was he still holding his gun? Lou wondered. What he did know was that this wasn't a man to trifle with. 'You'll get yours, One Eye,' he said as a parting shot.

'We all do, mister,' was the reply. Zachary

Concannon stepped to the bar and gave Joe
Malone twenty dollars on account and told him
he'd be staying a while.

'You watch him, Zachary,' Joe told him. 'He
works for Steven English who owns Top Hat,
biggest outfit around here. Sees himself taking
over, one day.'

'Really? How's he going to achieve that?'

'Steven only has one child, a daughter Clare.
Lou makes it pretty clear he's going to marry
her one day. She's a fine young woman, beautiful and intelligent, like her Ma. I reckon if you
invited all the young bucks who'd like to marry
Clare, here for a drink, you couldn't fit them all
in.'

'She sounds nice, hope she doesn't throw
herself away on that clown. Goodnight.' Zachary
threw his saddle-bags over his shoulder and
picked up his rifle. 'By the way,' he said, 'where
do I find Colonel Drake? I have to see him on
business.'

Joe hesitated. Hell, he thought, if I don't tell
him he'll find out elsewhere. 'Go out along the
creek. His is the first farm on the left, that you
come to.'

'Thanks, Joe. I don't mean him any harm. I
might be away for a few days. Keep my room for
me will you, please?'

'Sure enough, Zachary. What sort of business
are you in?'

Zachary Concannon paused. 'I'm a salesman.'

Joe Malone burst out laughing. 'What you're selling those farmers need, Zachary.'

Zachary smiled. 'Goodnight, Joe,' he said.

Charlie Abbott seemed to know when they would come. It was as though they waited until you thought they had given up, then they returned. They were back tonight.

'We said we'd be back, sodbuster!' someone yelled. Silence.

'Hello the house!' a new voice called.

'Go away, you bastards!' Charlie yelled back.

'I'm not here to hurt you Mr Abbott,' the new voice said. 'You and your family go back to bed; there'll be no more trouble. You have a nice farm here; it's a credit to you all.'

'Thank you,' Charlie called back. 'Goodnight.'

Louis Talbot had been hit over the head from behind. Now, here he was, hands shackled behind him. To his left he could see Red and Gus. 'What the hell happened?' he asked. The others didn't know; they had also been overpowered from behind. They dozed fitfully until the eastern sky brightened. Lou awoke. In front of him, he could see scuffed brown boots and denim trousers. He raised his head as much as he could and saw a blue cavalry cloak.

'You're dead, One Eye,' he croaked.

'Oh no, Mr Talbot,' Zachary Concannon replied, 'I'm just fine. But let's get one thing very clear: you give me any trouble I'll kill you. Now, how far to Top Hat ranch house?'

'Ten, twelve miles, north-east.'

'Good. I ran your horses off, so it's walk, I'm afraid.'

Chapter Two

It was mid-afternoon when Clare English tapped lightly on her father's office door and entered. Steven English sat back and looked at her. God, she was beautiful, the image of her mother, Margaret. She was 5'6" tall, 120 pounds, brown hair, brown, almond- shaped eyes. She had high cheekbones and a wide, sensuous mouth with well-formed lips. The only difference in the two women, apart from Margaret being exactly twice Clare's age which was twenty-two, was that Margaret was just starting to find a few grey hairs, much to her chagrin.

'Yes, baby?' Steven English asked.

'Sam asked me to get you, Daddy. He said come a-running, there's something you've got to see apparently.'

Steven English walked around his desk and put his arm around his daughter. 'Come on then,' he said, and kissed her on the head.

On the porch, Sam Lockwood, Steven's long-

time friend and foreman, stood staring to the
south. When Steven and Clare came out on to the
porch, Sam pointed and they looked. A hundred
yards out, plodding sluggishly up the slight rise to
the house, were three of the hands, followed along
by a rather ominous figure on a big horse.

'What the hell?' Steven muttered. To Clare he
said, 'Bring them to the office.'

Clare stood with Uncle Sam, and watched the
men approach. It was obvious they had walked a
long way and were very tired. Clare shifted her
attention to the man on the horse. He was tall and
wore an eye-patch. He doffed his hat with his left
hand.

'You must be Clare English,' he said. 'I was told
you're both beautiful and intelligent. I must say
that my informant is the master of the under-
statement, regarding your beauty, anyway.'

Clare inclined her head. 'Thank you, sir. What
do you want?'

'I'm afraid, as much as I'd like just to sit here
and talk to you, I must see your father.' Clare
stood aside and gestured to the door. The man
dismounted by throwing his right leg over his
horse's neck and slipping to the around. 'Go
ahead, boys,' he said to the hands.

For the first time, Clare noticed that they were
manacled. 'Stay close,' she said to Sam. The men
shuffled through the parlour and down the hall to
the office. Clare, walking at the rear, watched the
tall stranger. Unashamedly he inspected the

parlour as they passed through. They all entered
the office and stood before Steven English, who
was seated at his desk.

'I'm Zachary Concannon,' the stranger said
without preamble. 'Your men have been harassing
the farmers on Deer Creek; they will cease this
activity, immediately.'

Steven English couldn't believe what he was
hearing, in his own house, too. 'Just who the hell
are you?' he asked.

'I told you who, Mr English,' the tall man
replied. His hand came from under his cloak and
a silver disk floated through the air and landed
right in front of Steven. 'That's what I am.'

Steven picked up the disk. 'United States
Marshal,' he said. 'Well, well, those farmers got
themselves a pet lawman.'

'No, Mr English, the territory got itself a federal
lawman. I'm here to enforce the law, and your
men are breaking it.'

'I know nothing about it,' Steven English said.

Zachary Concannon smiled. 'Mr English, I'm
tired, hungry, and my eye hurts like hell, so let's
not dance around. You are the big squirrel up this
tree, so don't tell me you don't know what all the
other squirrels are doing.'

Steven English allowed himself just the hint of
a smile. 'So I know. Those people are on my land,
and I'll have them gone.'

'Mr English,' Zachary Concannon replied, 'get
this through your head, those farmers are on *their*

land. They homesteaded on public domain. It was never legally your land. They have fulfilled all the conditions of the Homestead Act and you cannot move them on. You should realize that all those men are veterans of a very successful army. If they mount an operation against you, they'll go through Top Hat like barley through a goose. If I can't sort this out, the army will come, and they'll do the same. You can't win, I'm afraid.'

Clare English was amazed at the forthrightness of this man. She watched as her father stood and moved to the window. 'My family settled this land, Marshal,' he said. 'We fought Indians, the elements, thieves of all kinds. I lost a brother and an uncle to the Indians, but we triumphed in the end. Now we're losing our land to farmers. Farmers, for God's sake!'

'I know, Mr English, and privately I sympathize with you, but government policy is to settle as many farming families as possible. Even if you had filed for ownership of all the land you considered to be yours, they wouldn't have let you have it. There are tens of thousands of families looking for their own little piece of dirt, so you big landowners had better get used to it, because it's the way of the future. Now you know how the Indians felt when you showed up.'

Steven English returned to his chair and sat thinking. Clare was fascinated by the clash of wills of these two men. To her surprise, Zachary Concannon started to move around the room inspecting items of which her father was very proud. There were flintlock rifles that had belonged to his grandfather who had fought in the revolutionary war, pistols, Indian war bonnets and weapons.

'Marvellous collection you have,' he commented. 'So, what's it to be?'

'All right, you win, unshackle my men.'

Now, to Clare's amazement, the marshal sat on the edge of her father's desk. 'Hell I'm tired,' he said, then returned his attention to her father. 'You don't understand, Mr English, these men are under arrest. They're guilty of destroying property. They burned down the Abbotts' barn, rode down their corn crop, and shot their cow. They also made unsavoury remarks to Mrs Abbott, who is a woman of considerable beauty.'

'We didn't insult her, boss,' Lou interjected.

Zachary Concannon turned on him. 'I was there, you idiot, have been every night for a fortnight, so shut up.' He returned his attention to Steven English. 'So, seeing as you knew your men were terrorizing these people and did nothing to stop it, you're guilty, too. Now, as there's no jail handy, I'm empowered to act as I see fit. So, for the damage they did, and the considerable anguish they caused this family, I fine your hands two hundred dollars each.'

'We ain't got that sort of money, One Eye,' Lou said.

'I thought of that too, Mr Talbot. Mr English

will pay your fines and collect from you, however he sees fit. Also, with winter coming on, the Abbotts will be desperate for their barn. Your fine, Mr English, is to replace all the lumber that was burnt, and to take your men down and help to rebuild it. Don't take these clowns, though.'

'And if I say no?' Steven English asked.

'Then I'll arrest you. I'll take you and your men to town and chain you to a post in the livery stables until I can get a judge here. Shouldn't take more than a month. In this lousy climate, you'll freeze to death in a week.'

Steven English laughed out loud. Clare could see that in some perverse way he was enjoying arguing with this strange man.

'You've sure got gall, Marshal, I'll give you that. You come into my home and tell me what I'll do? Amazing.'

'What's the alternative, Mr English? You going to sic that old gunfighter, who is no doubt lurking in the hallway, on to me? I doubt it. Apart from the fact you don't know how good I am with a gun – and I'm very good by the way – that's not your style. One thing I've learned in my six years as a marshal, is to read people. If I had to go against you, you'd be right there, doing your own killing, or getting killed, as the case may be.'

Steven English sat drumming his fingers on his desk. Clare moved to his side and draped an arm around his shoulders, not so much to comfort him, but so she could see this strange man as her father was seeing him. Her father reached up and squeezed her hand.

'Very well,' he said. 'I bow to progress. Your farmers may move on to my land in safety.'

Zachary smiled. 'They're not my farmers and it's not your land. Let's just say you won't stand in the way of progress. In fact, if you're smart, you could turn a good dollar from these new settlers. They need lumber and meat. Farmers grow grain that needs crushing. There are forty new families coming next spring, apparently. I'd set up a sawmill and a flourmill. If you can't beat them, you might as well profit from them.'

'Yes, we might as well. Will you unshackle my men now?'

'You'll pay their fines and your own fine?'

'Yes. I'll ride down in the next few days and take these geniuses to apologize.'

'Good.' The marshal moved behind Lou Talbot and undid one bracelet, then he handed Lou the keys and he undid himself and the others. 'Well, I must go,' Zachary said. 'It'll be dark before I get back to town. Dark and cold. How the hell do you stand it?'

'This cold is unseasonal, usually the weather is nice, this time of year,' Steven told him.

'Father, perhaps Marshal Concannon would like to stay to dinner and go to town tomorrow,' Clare said, out of the blue. After a short pause, Steven English said, 'Yes, good idea.'

'Why thank you, sir, Miss English, that would

be nice, and please call me Zachary.' They both nodded.

'Let me take your cloak,' Clare offered.

Everyone stood, stunned. Under his cloak, Zachary wore a sheepskin coat. The right sleeve was tucked into the pocket; the sleeve was empty from the elbow down. Lou Talbot and the other men burst out laughing.

'What the hell sort of marshal has one eye and one arm?' Lou enquired.

'The sort of marshal who took you three, Lou, and don't you forget it,' Clare replied, eager to come to Zachary's defence.

'Get out,' Steven English ordered. 'And don't think of running off before I get my money back.'

Clare took Zachary to the kitchen to meet her mother. Sam Lockwood entered the office and found Steven still at his desk.

'Well, what do you think?' Steven asked.

'He's a cool one, I'll give him that. Last time I stayed in town, I played cards with a whiskey drummer, loud-mouthed bastard. He said he'd been down in Abilene, Kansas, last year, and had seen the Beamon brothers shot to death by a marshal who only had one arm and one eye. I knew the Beamons when I . . . well, before I came to the mountains for my health. They were slippery bastards. Old Dirk never sat down without his gun on his lap, shot many a man without having to stand up. So if Concannon got 'em both, he's good, real good.'

'Have to be Concannon, I suppose.'

'Not many one-armed marshals around.'

'No,' Steven laughed. 'Damn it, I like his style, though.'

Zachary Concannon was introduced to Margaret English. Rather than sit in the parlour, he wanted to sit in the kitchen and smell the baking. Clare poured him coffee and got him warm water and a cloth to bathe his aching eye. She excused herself to take his horse to the barn. When she returned to the kitchen, she found her mother plying Zachary with hot cake. Clare noticed that he would hold the warm cloth to his eye, then very quickly cover it with his eye-patch. So, he was embarrassed about his eye, she thought. It was such a pity. Like a lot of tall men, his face was slightly angular, but he had a well-formed mouth and nose. His eye was blue, and his hair was fair and slightly curly. Clare concluded that before he'd been injured, he would have been a fine figure of a man.

When they went to the table, Zachary offered Clare his arm. 'Thank you, sir,' she responded, smiling coyly.

Margaret asked if he needed his meal cut up.

'Don't be embarrassed, Margaret,' Zachary told her. 'Yes, it's necessary, I'm afraid.'

Clare found Zachary to be a fine dinner companion. He was much travelled and well educated, which surprised her for some reason.

Over coffee, her father asked the question that she was sure they all wanted to ask. 'Where did you serve?'

'I served with Grant, in the Western campaign. But you really want to know where I was injured, don't you? It was at Cold Harbor, June 6th 1864. I lost my eye to a sabre cut, in hand-to-hand fighting. It punctured my eyeball apparently. I was coming out of the first-aid tent, when a shell exploded nearby, took my arm off clean as a whistle. It just wasn't my day.'

'What then? Did you go home?' Clare asked.

Zachary gave them a slightly sad, wistful smile. 'I was home, I'm from Virginia; Richmond to be exact. But in the sense you mean, no, I didn't go home. Couldn't really.'

'You're a Southerner and fought for the Union?' Clare asked.

'Lots of Southerners did, Clare. If you want to know why, I can't speak for others, but I didn't agree with slavery, pure and simple.' He paused and added sugar to his coffee and stirred slowly. Clare could see that this conversation upset him. 'My family were slave owners you see. Big plantation, huge house, fifty or sixty slaves. When I was a child, all my playmates were slave children. To me they were just children. If only all the world could be seen through the eyes of a child. The two best friends I've ever had were slaves, Ben and Josephine. They were brother and sister. When I was about fifteen, father sent me to Kentucky with one of the overseers, to buy horses. While I was away he sold them. I've never forgiven him, or had a civil conversation with him since.'

'Why do you blame yourself?' Clare asked.

Zachary paused before answering. 'I'd had an argument with father. I'm the eldest son, and he said that it wasn't seemly for me to be spending so much time with the slaves. I told him that I loved Jos, and that when I was old enough, I was going to marry her. Then he sent me to Kentucky and sold them.'

'But why?' Clare asked.

'Because he was their father,' Zachary blurted out. 'I was their half-brother. Tilly, their mother, told me. I suppose, when I was older, I'd have realized it. Tilly had been born on Truro. She was probably Father's playmate when they were children. When I remember back, I can still see them walking in the garden. See her put a hand on father's arm to call attention to something. Unheard of behaviour by a slave to her master. I can see Father pick her a flower. She was a regal-looking woman, still is.'

'Did your mother know?' Margaret English asked.

'I don't know. Mother's family were slave owners too, so perhaps the women just took it for granted that the men went with the slaves. I know you'll think this is a terrible thing to say, but my mother is the most useless woman I've ever met. I doubt I ever saw her out of bed before

mid-afternoon. The only time I ever saw her
excited, was if there was a ball, or a party. The
only time I saw her standing up during the day,
was when she was having a dress-fitting. Hell,
she's useless. How she ever got to have four children is beyond me. Well, I suppose it isn't, when
you consider that she spent most of her life in
bed. . . . Sorry, ladies,' Zachary added belatedly.
They laughed.

'How did your family survive the war?' Steven
asked.

'Not well. Like most Southerners, my father
was convinced the South would win. They didn't
have a clue. Supplies win wars, and most of the
manufacturing might was in the north. After the
war, of course, Confederate script was worthless;
my family was destitute, like everyone else. They
couldn't retain their land; I own it now. I went to
Father and told him that I could arrange to pay
off their debts through a banker I'd known in the
cavalry. The land had to be signed over to me.
Didn't help my relationship with my parents
when I told them I had absolutely no intention of
giving it back to them. I sold the big house and
two hundred acres, and made a handsome profit.
When I sold the mansion, I went upstairs and
tipped my mother out of bed and said, "Time to
get up, Mother". I have to admit that she's made a
fair fist of it since. She cooks, likes gardening. I
had modest houses built for them and my brother,
and any of our older people who stayed on. Tilly

married Cyrus, our former field foreman. I gave them a quarter section, on condition that Tilly doesn't help my mother in the house.'

'Who looks after everything for you?' Margaret asked.

'My younger brother Artemus, I made him my partner. He's twenty-three, six years younger than me. He's a frail lad, but very strong-willed and he knows farming. He has a marvellous wife, and he has Cyrus, of course, and some of the older men who stayed on.'

'How much land do you own?' Steven asked.

'A bit over three thousand acres.'

'Goodness me,' Clare said. 'Why are you a marshal then?'

'Several reasons. If I was home, all I'd do is argue with Father. Also, there's not a lot I could do on a farm besides bookwork. I make a good living doing what I do, and I play a lot of cards. A few times, the future of Truro has hung on the turn of a card. And I still hope to find Ben and Jos.'

They talked for an hour or more, until Steven and Margaret excused themselves and headed for bed. After an awkward silence, Clare asked Zachary if he would like to take a walk.

'Outside?' he asked in disbelief.

Clare laughed gaily. 'Of course outside, I love these cold nights.' Quite unbashfully, Clare walked on Zachary's left side and linked her arm through his. Zachary saw a slight glow from the direction of the barn. It looked like someone covering a cigarette with his hand. Someone was watching them, although Clare hadn't noticed.

'Can I ask why you're not married?' Zachary said hesitantly.

Clare laughed her marvellous laugh. 'Apart from the fact that I haven't met the man I want to marry yet, why should I be?'

'Well, most girls your age are. My two sisters are younger than you, they're both married. Must be a thousand men in the territory who would marry you tomorrow, if you wanted it.'

'Oh there are, don't worry. I even get proposals through the mail. I went to school back East, so I have lots of friends there. I suppose I've been back there, what, four times since I left school. There are always parties and I meet lots of men, all of whom think we were born to be together. Can I tell you how I really feel about marriage?'

'Yes.'

'Well, it may sound terribly vain, but it's really about how I feel about Top Hat. I love this land; I couldn't live anywhere else, not permanently anyway. Being an only child, I know that in the normal course of events, I'll inherit Top Hat one day. But, the way things are, when I do marry and eventually inherit, my husband will be known as the owner of Top Hat. So I could never marry anyone who didn't feel about the land as I do. Does that sound awful?'

'No, it sounds quite reasonable to me.'

They strolled leisurely to the house. Zachary

couldn't see if the watcher was still at the barn. In the house, Clare showed him his room.

'Well, goodnight,' she said, offering her hand.

Zachary held it. 'Goodnight and thank you. This has probably been the most pleasant evening I have ever had.'

Clare blushed profusely, 'Thank you, Zachary, I've enjoyed it tremendously too.'

After breakfast, when they all went out into the yard, they found all the men standing around and Lou holding Zachary's horse, saddled and ready to go.

'What are you all doing here?' Steven English asked.

'Come on, boss,' Lou replied. 'We're just havin' a bit of fun. We want to see how a one-armed man gets on his horse.'

Clare was about to object, but Zachary shook his head. 'Don't worry about it, Clare,' he told her and took the reins. He led the horse away and said, 'Lie down, Buck.' To everyone's surprise, the horse did exactly as he was told. 'That's how, Mr Talbot,' Zachary said. 'Now, if you think I can't ride and shoot at the same time.' Zachary wrapped the reins around the saddle horn and drew his revolver. He rode Buck around the yard guiding him only with his heels. The horse sped around, first one way then the other. 'Then if you think you can pull me off,' Zachary said, and the horse backed into the assembled hands and kicked furiously.

Clare clapped enthusiastically. 'That was marvellous, Zachary, can I ride him?'

Zachary explained that to get him to lie down, you just had to pull the reins back and down. To guide him, you used the pressure of your heels. Buck would turn away from your heel. To make him kick, just exert pressure in front of the girth.

'Why does that make him kick?' Clare asked.

'I've always assumed he's ticklish,' Zachary replied. Clare looked dubious. 'Imagine if someone tickled you under the arms, what would happen?' Zachary asked.

'Father would shoot him,' she replied.

Zachary laughed. 'Other than that, you'd struggle, wouldn't you? Well, this is how Buck struggles.' Clare put Buck through all his tricks as the hands looked on. She volunteered to ride part of the way with Zachary, and went to the barn for her own horse. To mount this time, Zachary just swung aboard, very athletic for a big man on to a big horse.

They rode silently for half an hour. 'I'd best go back now,' Clare said eventually.

'All right,' Zachary replied. Then, 'Look, Colonel Drake is having a barn dance on Saturday night, and I've been invited. Would you care to accompany me?'

Clare asked, 'Why do you think I'd do that?'

Zachary was flustered. 'Why does a young lady

ever accept an invitation from a man? She either finds him attractive, interesting, or she would just like to go out for the evening. All things considered, I'll settle for number three.'

Clare hoped she was hiding her excitement, 'All right, Zachary, I'd like that, thank you.'

'That's great,' Zachary replied. 'I'll pick you up mid-afternoon. I was asked to stay over, so if you wish to, bring whatever you need.'

'I'll see you then.' Clare reined her horse away. 'Zachary, I wouldn't discount reasons one and two if I were you,' she called, and drove her horse into a gallop.

Clare was feeling unusually happy as she unsaddled her horse in the barn. Was it this strange man? She had never seen anyone stand up to her father the way Zachary had.

Wherever Clare went, men wanted to impress her with their charm and wit, but Zachary hadn't needed to try. He had talked about himself certainly, but it hadn't been bragging. It was just an extremely interesting story of a man's life, one who had suffered a lot, emotionally and physically, but who hadn't let his injuries deter him from life in any way. Her musings were interrupted when someone grabbed her by the arm, startling her greatly.

'What the hell do you think you're doin'?' Lou Talbot asked angrily.

Clare pulled away. 'What are you talking about, Lou?'

'One Eye, that's what. You're throwin' yourself at him and I don't like it. You're my girl, hear? My girl.'

Clare turned her horse into its stall. 'Lou,' she said, 'we've had this conversation a dozen times, but I'll tell you once again: I'm not your girl and I never will be. I like you as a friend, but our friendship is being sorely taxed by how you behave. I have never given you any reason to think this way. And if you ever mention this again I'll tell Father, and you'll be on the trail in a flash, is that clear?'

'Yes, Clare.'

'Good. I suggest that you think about moving on in the Spring. Until then, keep your nose out of my affairs.'

'I've been here twelve years,' Lou protested.

'Then it's time for a change, Lou.'

Lou watched Clare leave the barn. He turned and found himself face to face with Sam Lockwood. 'You spyin' on me, Sam?'

'You leave Clare alone, boy, you hear?' Sam said menacingly.

Lou tried to tough it out, 'You want her too, do you, old man? Then I suggest you get rid of that half a marshal.'

Sam drove a left fist into Lou's stomach, then dropped him with a crisp right to the jaw. As Lou struggled to his knees, Sam grabbed his hair and pulled his face up to meet his own. 'You listen to me, boy,' he hissed. 'These people are the closest thing to family I'll ever have. Clare is the closest thing to a daughter I'll ever have. You touch her again and I'll kill you, is that clear, you loud-mouthed little shit?'

'Yes,' Lou managed to say.

Sam let him go. 'Clare gave you some good advice, boy, only don't wait until Spring: move out now.'

Chapter Three

Clare prepared for the dance with great anticipation. She decided to wear a blue dress that she had bought on her last trip to New York in the spring. It was her special occasion dress. She hadn't worn it until today. Much to her surprise, Zachary wore a three-piece black suit. He stood in the parlour, hat in hand, his cloak around his shoulders.

'You look breathtaking,' he told her.

Clare blushed slightly. 'Thank you, Zachary,' she replied.

Clare was prepared to stay at the Drakes' overnight, so Zachary put her bag in the buggy he had rented for the occasion. Steven English and his wife stood on the porch and watched them leave. 'They make a lovely couple,' Margaret remarked.

Her husband put his arm around her shoulder. 'That they do, sweetheart.'

Clare offered to drive and Zachary handed her the reins. As they passed the bunkhouse, Zachary saw Lou Talbot watching them; he could feel the man's animosity. 'Lou smoke?' he asked.

'What a strange question. Yes, he does, why?'

'I reckon he was watching us the other night when we took that stroll you invited me on.' Clare didn't answer. 'Is he interested in you?'

'Unfortunately, Lou has plans for me that I don't care about.'

'I see. Would you like me to slap him over the head? Shoot him? Anything?'

'No thank you, I can handle it.' They talked and laughed all the way to the Drake's farm. It seemed as though all the Deer Creek farmers were there, along with their children. When Zachary assisted Clare down from the buggy, some people stood and stared at her with scarcely disguised antagonism.

Colonel and Mrs Drake welcomed them effusively. Still, the others stared. Zachary took Clare's hand, 'This is Clare English,' he said to the watchers. 'She is here as my guest.'

People began to drift away. A girl about Clare's age hurried up and held out her hand. 'I'm Susan Drake, Clare. I'm so pleased that you could come. Let's put your things in the house.' The two young women walked away chatting freely.

A couple with two children approached Zachary. The man introduced himself as Charlie Abbott. 'We want to thank you for what you did for us, Marshal,' the man said. 'How did you know when to come?'

'I was there every night for a fortnight, Charlie. Patience usually pays off. Did Mr English come to see you?'

'Yes, sir. He paid us six hundred dollars and his men will be down to finish the barn next week. Actually he was very nice. We talked things over, I suppose we'd be angry too, in his place.'

Zachary moved among the farmers being introduced by Colonel Drake. Most people couldn't resist a furtive glance at the empty sleeve stuck into the pocket of his coat. Zachary couldn't find Clare so he went to the house. He knocked and Susan let him in. 'Susan's getting married soon,' Clare said. 'Isn't her dress lovely?'

'Yes, it is. So, is this an engagement party?'

'Kind of,' Susan replied sheepishly. Zachary gave her a twenty-dollar gold piece from himself and Clare. Later in the evening, Zachary seemed to disappear. Clare found him by the fire. 'What are you doing?' she asked.

'Warming up. This is the warmest I've been in a month.'

Clare sat with him, 'We haven't danced yet,' she said.

'You're doing all right with all those farmers.'

Clare laughed. 'You're embarrassed about your arm, right?'

'Not really,' Zachary replied. 'I've long since got used to the fact that it will never grow back. What embarrasses me is that people get embarrassed. If I ask ladies to dance, they usually don't know whether to laugh or cry, so I don't ask anymore.'

'You invited me, now you'll dance. Come on, up.'

'All right, but not dances where we change partners or have to whirl around quickly. You'll go spinning off on your own.'

'Well, I'll just have to hang on extra tight, or you will have to put your arm around me.'

They arrived back at Top Hat shortly after noon, Clare invited Zachary to lunch, but he declined. 'There's a dance next Saturday night, would you like to go to that?' he asked.

'We usually go as a group,' Clare replied. 'I'll meet you.'

'All right, thanks for last night,' Zachary replied, then reined the horse around and drove out of the yard.

Word that Zachary had escorted Clare English to a dance spread like wildfire. People grinned knowingly when he walked by. Joe Malone called him a wily old dog. Zachary didn't quite know what that meant. Some drovers passing through town, reported to Joe that there had been a killing at Dyson's, could he tell the marshal. He did so. 'Just keep going out along Deer Creek,' Joe informed Zachary. He set out on Tuesday morning, pleased to get away from the town for a time. Late morning found him at Charlie Abbott's place. To his surprise, he had to admit, some of the Top Hat hands were working on the barn under the direction of Steven English. Zachary rode up and sat watching.

'Checking on us are you, Zachary?' Steven asked.

'No, just passing through on my way to Dyson's. How far is it?'

'Hurry along and you'll make it by tonight. What's wrong?'

'Been a killing, don't know the details.'

'Miserable bastard, that Dyson. Want to stay to lunch?'

'No thanks, I won't. Just one thing: it's probably none of my business, but from talking to Clare, I think she's being harassed by Lou Talbot.'

'In what way?'

'Come on, Steven, how does a man harass a woman? Clare is very beautiful and your only child. Think about it, I'm sure you'll work it out. Be better if you didn't tell her I told you though.'

'Better for who? You or Clare?' Steven asked with a smile.

Zachary smiled back. 'You're a smart man, Steven, you'll work that out, too.' Zachary dug Buck in the ribs and continued on.

Clare came from the house. 'Was that Zachary?' she asked breathlessly. 'Why didn't he stay?' They both watched Zachary disappearing into the distance. 'He could have passed the time of day, at least.'

Her father put his arm around her, 'That's how he is, baby. Many lawmen lead lonely lives, force of circumstances, I suppose. Zachary, well, he seems lonelier than most, I'll admit. I think, from the way he has acted since we met him, you know, just turning up and laying the law down the way he did, not knowing whether he'd be shot to pieces, he feels that he has to keep proving himself.'

'He doesn't have to prove anything to me, Daddy,' Clare said.

Her father gave Clare a squeeze. 'Not to you, darling. Given his physical disabilities, I believe that he has to prove himself to himself; yes, I believe that.'

The Top Hat men worked diligently on the barn until Thursday and by mid-afternoon, it was all but finished.

Steven and Clare were standing in the yard when a hand called, 'Boss!' and pointed west. A few hundred yards out, Zachary came riding, wrapped in his cloak. Steven had to admit that he looked daunting, evil almost. A dark apparition on a huge horse.

Zachary reined in and tipped his hat to Clare, 'Good afternoon,' he said. He seemed terribly tired.

'What happened at Dyson's?' Steven asked.

'The son Alan shot his father. The old man had a habit of beating his wife, apparently. Poor woman had the best black eye and busted lips I've ever seen.'

'Oh, my God,' Clare declared. 'What will happen

to Alan? What will happen to Mrs Dyson and the girls?'

'Nothing. I'll write it up as justifiable homicide. My only regret is that I didn't get to shoot the old bastard myself.'

'And that's that?' Clare asked.

'Yes, that's that,' Zachary replied rather shortly. 'This is what I do, Clare, I enforce the law as I see it. There was no point in arresting the boy. Besides, the girl Mary threatened to shoot me if I did.'

Clare and her father laughed. 'She's twelve years old, Zachary,' Clare informed him.

'Might be, but she knows how to use a shotgun, believe me.'

'What did you do to her?'

'I kicked her ass and fined her fifty cents and enough sandwiches to get me home.' Clare and Steven laughed again.

Clare offered Zachary coffee, and went to the house when he accepted.

'I got waylaid by a bunch of riders and someone named Quentin Quirk, do you know him?' Zachary asked.

'Yes, they are our western neighbours. We're very friendly; they've been here as long as we have. Was he a young man?' Zachary nodded. 'That's Quentin junior. He has political ambitions, wants to be the first governor of Montana, has a while to wait, I think. We see them at Christmas, Thanksgiving, times like that. Clare saw a lot of him when they were both at school in the East. Was a time we thought, you know, he's an only son, Clare's an only daughter. Quentin senior would like nothing better than to get his hooks into Top Hat.' The two men talked for twenty minutes. In that time a wagon full of young people had arrived and Clare seemed engrossed in talking to them. 'I think I'll go,' Zachary said eventually. 'That coffee seems to be coming via Mexico.'

Steven looked at the group around Clare, 'Sorry,' he said.

'No matter. Thanks for living up to your word.'

'Think I wouldn't?' Steven asked.

'Not really. You didn't know your men were rousting these people, did you?' Steven shook his head. 'But you should have.'

Steven laughed, 'Yes, I should have.'

Zachary gave him a slight smile then rode off. 'I'll send a rider to check on Dyson occasionally!' Steven yelled after him. Zachary raised his hand in acknowledgement.

'Damn him,' Clare said when she finally arrived. 'I got him coffee and he just rode off.'

'You went half an hour ago, girl. It was obvious that you preferred being sweet talked by those farm boys. I wouldn't have waited either.'

'Sorry, Father,' Clare replied, blushing at his admonition.

The dance was all but over when Clare realized that Zachary wasn't coming. Not that she had missed any dances; she had been besieged by young men from the farming settlement. She enquired of Mr Castle, the store owner and mayor, where she could find the marshal. He informed her that Zachary worked out of the saloon. 'A chair by the fire,' he said with a chuckle.

Zachary was indeed by the fire, playing poker with two salesmen. Zachary saw the man opposite him staring at someone behind him, he turned and saw Clare looking rather uncertain of herself among the drinkers and clamour of the saloon. 'Deal me out for a minute,' Zachary said.

'What are you doing in here?' he asked Clare.

'You said you'd meet me at the dance,' she replied softly.

'Well, I didn't think I'd want to stand around like a dog waiting to be thrown a bone, while you danced with everyone else.'

Clare averted her eyes. 'I'm sorry,' Zachary said.

'No, I'm sorry,' Clare said, 'I didn't do this very well.'

Zachary went to the table and got his money. One man objected to his leaving, he wanted a chance to get his money back.

'Mister,' Zachary said, 'we'll be here forever; I suggest that you change to checkers, poker isn't your game. Goodnight.'

Clare was cold, so Zachary put his cloak around her shoulders and they went back to the church hall. The band had just started to play a waltz, and people stared when Zachary put his arm around Clare and she put her arms around him.

They had barely started when Lou Talbot tapped Zachary on the shoulder. 'I'm cuttin' in,' he said.

'Don't do this, Lou, please,' Clare asked.

'I insist,' Lou replied. 'Ol' One Eye here is a Virginia gentleman, did you know that, Clare? He knows it ain't polite to start a scene, don't you, One Eye?'

Zachary stood aside and bowed slightly to Clare, 'Goodnight, Clare, thank you.' To Lou he said, 'I should have followed my first instinct and shot you when I had the chance.'

Lou grinned triumphantly as he whirled Clare away while everyone watched. Zachary collected his cloak and left. 'I'll never forgive you for this, Lou, never. I'm going to talk to father, so start packing,' Clare spat.

'You're mine, you hear?' Lou said equally forcefully. 'You're mine. Your old man won't get rid of me, and you ain't throwin' yourself away on some half man, is that clear?'

As soon as the music stopped, Clare pulled away from Lou, 'You stay away from me, you bastard,' she told him, then stormed off leaving him alone.

Mid-morning on Sunday, Lou was summoned to Steven English's office. Steven was standing at the window, and didn't turn around when Lou said, 'You want me, boss?'

Steven sat at his desk, 'You're harassing Clare, Lou, why?'

'She's throwin' herself at that marshal and I won't have it. She's my girl, you oughta tell her it's time we got wed.'

Steven burst out laughing. 'Are you out of your mind?' he asked. 'I wouldn't try telling her who to marry even if I could. I certainly won't make her marry you.'

'You don't think I'm good enough, do you?' Lou yelled.

'No!' Steven yelled back. 'But don't take it personally, I don't think anyone is. Fathers feel that way, I suppose.' He rose and went to the door and called, 'Sam!'

Sam Lockwood appeared from nowhere, 'Yes, Steven?' he asked.

'See Lou off the place, please.'

Sam smiled, 'Pleasure,' he replied. Sam stood as Lou saddled his horse, 'Bye bye, big mouth,' he said, as Lou mounted his horse and spurred it into a run.

Chapter Four

Zachary was at his desk writing reports and a few letters. In his letter to his superiors, he suggested that this part of the territory needed a marshal and a deputy. He suggested that they be sent by December at the latest, as he would like to move on shortly after Christmas. He also informed them that he would like to go to the west coast and down to California. He heard a commotion and turned to see Sam hurrying towards him. 'Lou Talbot kidnapped Clare,' Sam said breathlessly.

Zachary sat, dumbfounded. 'You sure?' he asked. Of course Sam was sure. Clare had been out with Slim Hunt, one of the hands, when Lou had come upon them. He had threatened Clare at gunpoint. When Slim had tried to intervene, Lou had wounded him and taken Clare with him. They were headed into the mountains.

'We're going after them. When we get him, we'll hang the bastard, Zachary, any objections?'

Zachary shook his head as Sam turned to leave.

'Sam,' Zachary said. Sam turned as Zachary reached into his saddle-bags, bringing out a deputy's badge. He threw it to Sam. 'Might as well be legal.' Sam smiled and left. Zachary went and told Joe.

'Shit,' Joe said.

'Shit's right,' Zachary replied. He asked were there any old-timers around who could give him an opinion as to where someone would run. Joe told him to go and see Amos Allnut, who lived in a cabin on the edge of town. 'He was here before God,' Joe told him. 'He's almost blind and must be ninety, but he's smart as a whip, still. An interesting old man.' Zachary took a bottle of whiskey and walked down to the cabin. A surprisingly strong voice bade him to come in.

Amos Allnut was sitting by the fire in his neat, one-roomed cabin. His face was withered up like a walnut and was the colour of old leather. His snow-white hair reached right past his shoulders. Zachary introduced himself and poured drinks for them both as they sat by the fire. He told the old man what had happened and asked his opinion as to where Lou would run.

'Tell me what you think, son,' Amos said.

'Well, I wouldn't go into the mountains this time of the year. He couldn't have provisioned himself for a winter; this is a spur-of-the-moment thing. I'd head to where I could find shelter and buy food without drawing attention to myself. Where's that? It would have to be a big town. Butte?'

Amos smiled and held out his glass, 'You didn't need me, son.'

'You think he'll head for Butte?'

'Yep, only place he can go. Plenty of old miners' shacks and line camps, places like that. He'll reckon that people will follow him into the mountains. It's snowing up there now so his tracks will get covered up quick. By now he's headed southwest as fast as he can go. If I was you, I wouldn't even track him. I'd go straight to Butte; you'll get him. When you do, shoot him once for me.'

As Zachary left, he put fifty dollars on the table and told the old man to buy some supplies for the winter.

Zachary went to the store and bought coffee, jerky and biscuits. He told Joe Malone he'd be out of town for a few days. Joe gave him a bottle of whiskey. 'For the chills.' Then, he went to the livery and asked for the use of another horse.

The livery man knew why. 'Take mine,' he said.

'I'll ride him and lead Buck for the rest of the day. Probably get twenty miles. If I let him loose will he come home?'

'If he don't, someone will bring him back,' the man told him. 'If I was you, I'd take the old wagon road to Butte. It's three days by wagon. Push it you'll be there by tomorrow night.'

Zachary tied Buck to the saddlehorn, mounted and headed out.

By late Tuesday, Zachary had reached Butte.

He doubted that Lou could be here before him. He resisted the urge to go into the town to find a bed, and settled down in the lee of some rocks. So his wait began. Wednesday came and went and doubt started to play on Zachary's mind. He has to have food, he kept telling himself. On Thursday, it started to snow. Zachary watched the trail from sun-up. Late morning, still nothing. Then, there he was, coming in from the north, in a line of trees that were west of the trail.

Zachary was now faced with a dilemma. Did he wait for Lou and then follow him? Or did he follow his trail? He decided that he would rather get him before he returned to his hideout, so there was no danger to Clare. But, if he followed Lou's trail, Lou would see his tracks and be instantly suspicious. He decided to head out on the trail to town, then go across country until he cut Lou's tracks.

When Zachary finally spotted Lou's trail in the snow, he was above it, so he turned back and continued on north some more, before again turning west. A few miles on, the trail was harder to see as it was snowing, but Zachary breasted a small hill and there it was. A small hut, barely discernible with its covering of snow. Through his telescope, Zachary could see a wisp of smoke rising from the chimney. In a tumbledown lean-to, he saw another horse. It looked like Clare's.

Zachary was overwhelmed by the desire to rush to the cabin and see to Clare's welfare, but he

restrained himself. He would do nothing to alert
Lou. He wanted this matter finished now. He tied
Buck in the trees then walked to the lean-to and
settled down to wait. He sat on the remnants of a
manger which made a passable armchair. In the
shadows, he doubted that Lou would see him,
unless he looked directly at him. His thoughts
returned to Clare: was she injured? Would this
experience haunt her for the rest of her life? He'd
seen women who had been abducted and molested
by men before. With some, there had been no
outward sign of injury; others, well, at worst they
were just shadows of their former selves. One he
had seen, just sat, never to utter another word,
condemned to spend her life in an asylum. The
depth of feeling he had for Clare startled him.

The tethered horse whinnied restlessly.
Zachary could hear the soft footfalls of another
horse, coming through the snow. Lou dismounted
outside and led his horse into the shelter. A sack
of supplies hung over the front of his saddle. He
was about to unsaddle his horse when Zachary
cocked his .45, the noise deafening in the confines
of the lean-to.

'Hands up, Lou, turn around real slow,' Zachary
said.

Lou did as he was bid. 'Well, One Eye, how'd you
find me?'

'Quite easily, Lou; you had to get food, it had to
be here – simple. Is Clare all right?'

'Yeah, I wouldn't hurt her. I love her.'

'Shit, Lou, you kidnapped her. How can you say that?'

'Things were fine 'til you came along. All we need is some time together and things'll be fine again.'

'No, they won't, Lou. She doesn't love you and that's all there is to it. My coming along had nothing to do with it.'

Realization dawned in Lou's eyes. 'You take me back and they'll hang me,' he whispered.

'Yes, they will, Lou.'

Lou went for his gun. Zachary raised his and shot him twice through the chest. Lou went over backwards against his horse and, already dead, slid slowly to the ground. With little caution, Zachary hurried to the cabin and went in. Clare was bound and gagged and lying on a cot. Her fear-filled eyes brimmed over with tears when she saw him. As quickly as he could, Zachary untied her and removed the gag. He sat on the edge of the bed and held her as she cried hysterically. After a time, her sobs subsided.

'Is he dead?' she asked into Zachary's neck. Zachary nodded. Again, Clare was silent.

'Are you all right?' Zachary asked. 'Did he. . . .' He couldn't ask the question.

'Yes, I'm all right, and, yes, he did,' Clare responded aggressively. Then, 'I'm sorry, I shouldn't be yelling at you.'

'You yell, scream, hit me, whatever you like,' Zachary said.

'God, Zachary, what will I do?'

Zachary held her at arm's length. 'Now you listen to me,' he said softly but sternly. 'You will get over this, you will. I don't pretend to know how you feel, but I've seen this before and you will get over it. You have the support of your family and friends, and you will go on with your life. I command it.'

Clare managed a smile. 'Yes, Zachary, and thank you for coming for me. Deep down I knew that you would.'

'Your father and all the hands are out, too.'

'Yes, but for some reason I knew you'd find me.'

Zachary stood. 'Well, we must move on. It's snowing like hell out there. We'll go to town and send a message to your parents. Then we'll get you some clean clothes and a bath, and decide what to do.'

'I just want to go home.'

'I know, but we might have to sit out this storm, all right?' Clare nodded.

Zachary sent Clare to get Buck while he saddled her horse and, with difficulty, got Lou's body up on to his own horse and tied him on. Clare was shaken at the sight of Lou draped across his saddle. 'Can't leave him,' Zachary told her. Clare rode Buck. She spent time riding him in and out of the trees, guiding him with her heels. Zachary was happy for her, he could see that eventually, she would recover from her ordeal.

*

People stood and stared as Zachary and Clare rode down Main Street: a beautiful young woman and a dour-looking man, leading a horse with a body draped across the saddle. The sheriff was out on to the sidewalk before Zachary had helped Clare down.

'What the hell's this?' he asked. Zachary introduced himself and Clare and showed his badge.

'Heard you was in the territory,' the sheriff said.

Zachary explained to the sheriff what had happened. Then he and Clare took their horses to the livery stable, and continued on to the telegraph office and sent messages to Clare's parents. Zachary's message read: *Clare safe and well. Lou dead. Will return when weather permits. Be prepared to offer much love and support.* He hoped by asking for support, they'd be able to read between the lines and realize what had happened. Clare was at a loss as to what to say.

'Just say something personal,' Zachary told her.

Her message was, *Dearest Mom and Dad. Am safe and well, thanks to Zachary. We'll start for home when we can. I hope it's soon; I miss you so much and I'm sick of listening to Zachary complain about the weather. Love Clare.*

'You don't mind do you?' Clare asked.

Zachary smiled. 'No, I don't mind. Besides, it's true.'

Clare hugged him and kissed him on the cheek. 'You're a lovely man, Zachary,' she informed him.

They bought clothes then booked into a hotel.

Zachary asked for adjoining rooms. The clerk leered at Clare. Zachary grabbed him by the shirt and said, 'Don't even think it, you bastard.'

After baths and a leisurely dinner, Clare retired to bed. She asked Zachary to leave the door between their rooms open.

Zachary woke in the middle of the night and heard her crying. He stood at the door between their rooms, not knowing what to do. 'You all right?' he asked.

'No,' she snuffled in reply.

'Can I come in?'

'Yes.' The bed groaned, as she reached out to turn up the lamp.

Zachary sat on the bed, 'What's wrong?' he asked.

'Everything, Zachary, everything,' Clare replied. 'What if I'm pregnant, what will I do?'

'People will know what happened, Clare, you can't be blamed.'

'Can't I? I was in school with a girl who got pregnant. She was sneaking out at night to see this boy. He got her drunk and raped her. Do you think everyone understood? Hardly. Her parents sent her away to have her baby. Her mother said she should have killed herself rather than let this fellow touch her. Killed herself, God!'

Zachary took her hand. 'Your parents aren't like that.'

'No, they're not, but everyone else is. Everyone likes to see people in our position fall. The great Clare English, heiress, with her bastard child.'

'You can rise above what anyone thinks, Clare.
You're a great lady; no one will break your spirit,
no one.'

In the soft light, Clare smiled and squeezed his
hand. 'Thank you, Zachary. Do you know what the
worst of it is? He was very gentle and he told me
that he loved me. In other circumstances, I might
have enjoyed it. Some of the girls I knew in school,
all they could talk about was what it would be
like. As you get older you wonder about it. Wonder
when you meet a man you like, will it be him.
What upsets me the most, apart from the fact that
I might be pregnant, is that I'll never get to choose
who I give myself to. I shall never forgive Lou for
that. Does that sound awful?'

'No. A young lady should get to choose. What a
woman can give a man is the greatest gift imag-
inable. And it's not unnatural for you to think
about it; men do, why shouldn't women?'

'This sounds like the voice of experience talking,' Clare said with a slight smile. 'Have you been
with a woman, Zachary?'

'That's hardly the question a lady asks, Clare,'
Zachary replied, trying to be stern.

Clare actually laughed. This was good, Zachary
thought.

'Oh come on, Zachary,' Clare said. 'I'm baring
my soul, my innermost feelings, the least you can
do is reciprocate.'

Zachary laughed. 'All right, yes, I have. More
than a few times if you must know.'

'Aha,' Clare said almost gleefully. 'So, tell me about your first conquest.' Zachary just looked at her. 'If you don't, I'll return to being sad and morose.'

'Very well. Her name was Alice O'Connell and her parents owned a store in Richmond. I didn't really conquer her, it was the other way round, actually. In those days, before the war, I suppose you'd have to say that I was a good catch. Oldest son, heir to a big plantation. I was big and strong for my age – I was eighteen at the time. Alice was a few years older than me, but I liked her a lot. At that age, you think it's flattering to be chased by a very popular girl. I was old enough to know that mothers were looking for husbands for their daughters. Whenever there was a ball or a party, mothers would come and put their case to my father, no matter what I thought.'

'You're digressing, Zachary.'

'Yes, I am a bit. So, I went to a party with Alice. When I took her home, she sneaked me to her room and we did the deed.'

'Weren't you worried she'd get pregnant?'

'My first thought, believe me. But Alice assured me that everything would be all right. We were really good friends until the war started, when I was nearly twenty. Just before I went off to enlist, I saw her. She thought it was so romantic. She said I'd come home a Confederate hero, we'd marry and live happily ever after. I said that sounded nice. The trouble was, I was going to fight

for the Union and I thought the South was going
to get a belting. That was the fastest I ever got out
of bed, I tell you.'

'Did you ever see her again?'

'Yes, I saw her after the war. I went into the
store and she was there. Her father had been
killed serving with the Citizens Volunteer
Militia. She had married a local boy whose father
owned a stock agency. She had two of the loveli-
est little girls.' Zachary paused, thinking. Clare
waited for him to continue. 'What struck me, was
how dignified she was. There was hardly
anything in the store, but Alice made cakes and
bread and jams, things like that. She wore a ging-
ham dress that had been washed so often all the
colour was gone, but it was spotless. The store
was as neat as a pin and her children were beau-
tifully mannered. Her husband was working like
hell to get the stock agency going again. The
whole thing was just so sad. They were having a
hard time trying to make something of their
lives, but when she saw me, she cried. Shit. She
had no idea how often the thought of her kept me
warm on a cold night during the war. Life's not
fair, is it?' he asked, then smiled. 'No point me
telling you that, is there?'

'What happened then?'

'I lent them ten thousand dollars and put them
in contact with people they could buy supplies
from. They had a bit of trouble at first, but when
people found out that I was their partner, they

were left alone. I'm reputed to be very violent with a short fuse.'

'So? Tell me all. How come?'

'Well, I suppose I got a reputation for being violent just after the surrender. I was at home then. A few days after I arrived home, looters came to Truro. They were Union soldiers on their way home and they weren't going home empty-handed. Their leader assumed I was a Rebel, of course. He said, "You'll have to shoot us, to stop us", so I did, shot him anyway, and wounded another. They ran off when my brother and Cyrus turned up. After that, I don't know, I suppose I do have a short fuse, especially if anyone is trying to take advantage of my family, or any of our people. Carpetbaggers think it's their God-given right to take everything. Although my brother Artemus is very strong-willed, people have tried by fair means and foul to force him off our land. When they try, he sends for me. I've slapped quite a few over the head. Doesn't happen a lot now. Apparently, Artemus just says I'm on my way home and that fixes things pretty quick.'

They talked on until dawn. It seemed to Zachary that the more they talked, the easier it was to make her laugh. As dawn broke, Clare seemed weary and Zachary said he would leave her to sleep.

'Thank you, Zachary,' she said. 'People who think you're violent, don't know you very well. You're a kindly, gentle person and I'll never forget what you've done for me. Doesn't solve my problem though, does it?' she concluded wryly.

After a short pause Zachary said, 'Clare, there is a simple solution to what you see as your problem.'

'Which is?' she asked tentatively.

'You could marry me.'

Clare looked at him disbelievingly. 'Zachary, I don't know what to say. I . . . I don't love you, Zachary, but I like you very much. In time who knows? But I don't love you, I'm sorry.'

Zachary gave her a gentle smile, 'I know, and believe me, marriage isn't something I saw on my horizon. But it solves your problem. If we get married immediately and you're pregnant, who's to know it isn't mine? Only you and me. If you're not, well, I'll be moving on in a few months. In either case, you can be the deserted wife and divorce me. You won't be the only divorced woman in the world. But it has to be now; everyone can count up to nine. When will you know for sure?'

'Well, I'm very erratic; could be anything up to six weeks.'

Zachary stood. 'Well, think about it. A few days no one will notice, but five or six weeks . . . I don't know, it's up to you.' He kissed her on the forehead. 'Get some sleep.'

Clare didn't wake until noon. She looked troubled and wanted to talk. Zachary insisted that she have something to eat first. He sat by the fire, while she paced nervously around the small parlour. Concentrating on looking out the window, Clare asked, 'Zachary, why? What's in it for you, if I do marry you?'

'Not a lot, Clare,' he replied. 'It's just, well, with the war and all, I've seen enough lives ruined by circumstances beyond people's control. I like you very much, and I don't want to see your life ruined. Besides, if I live to be old and grey, I'll have the satisfaction of knowing that I was once married to a lovely woman, even if it was only for a short time. I don't expect anything from you; it would be a marriage in name only.'

Clare continued to stare out the window for a time, then she turned towards him, 'Very well,' she whispered.

They were married that afternoon by a justice of the peace. Two days later, they started for home, first thing in the morning. Clare was regaining her vitality and asked if she could ride Buck. She enjoyed riding him in and out of the trees. 'Go easy on him,' Zachary told her. 'By the time we get home, he'll have travelled twice as far as needs be.' Clare laughed and drove the horse around in a figure eight.

Chapter Five

When they were in sight of Top Hat ranch house, they could see Steven English in the yard, talking to some of the hands. Clare drove Buck into a gallop. Her father saw her and ran to the house to get his wife, and they both raced to meet her. Zachary ambled along to give them time alone. Clare and her mother went to the house and Steven waited for Zachary.

'I don't know what to say,' he said emotionally.

'It's my job, Steven, forget it.'

'Are you going to stay the night?'

'Steven, you'd better talk to Clare, then I'm sure you'll want to talk to me.'

Steven looked at him questioningly. 'OK, come in.'

One of the hands took the horses and the two men went to the house. Zachary sat by the fire until Steven reappeared. He went straight to a cabinet by the wall. 'Whiskey?' he asked.

'Thank you.'

Steven drank hastily, then poured another. As Zachary sat, Steven stared into the fire. 'Shit,' he said eventually. 'How did you know where to go?'

'I hunt men, Steven; I'm very good at it.'

Steven turned. 'You should have told me,' he said angrily.

'Why? A dozen men couldn't have got him any sooner. Sometimes one man can accomplish more than an army. I won't apologize for what I did.'

Steven gave him a slight smile. 'I'm sorry. You were right to do what you did. Hardly the time for hurt pride, is it?'

'Natural feelings of a father, I suppose.'

'So, what happens now, Zachary?'

'Nothing. Clare will live here; I'll live in town. If anyone asks why, we'll say I don't want my wife living in a saloon. When she's in town she can visit me, and I'll visit here. No one will realize anything is wrong, until I just ride away.'

'Why are you doing this, Zachary?' Steven asked. Zachary just looked at him. 'Well, well,' Steven continued, 'You love her, by God, you love her. Does she know?'

'No, and you won't tell her.'

'But why? We know she likes you a lot; hell, *we* even like you. Why not—?'

'No!' Zachary replied firmly. 'Don't say anything. If things work out, fine; if not, then in the new year I'm gone. Clear?'

Zachary returned to town the next day. It was obvious that word had got around that he had rescued Clare. In the saloon there was much back slapping and good wishes. Joe took Zachary to his office for a quiet drink. On the desk, were a pair of pistols and a flintlock rifle. 'What's all this?' Zachary asked.

'Amos Allnut left them for you. There's a letter, too,' Joe said. When Zachary looked at him questioningly, Joe continued, 'He's dead, Zachary. He took his own life, froze to death.' On the day Zachary left for Butte, Joe said, old Amos had come into the saloon. He had bought himself a new suit and a white shirt with a starched collar. He had rented a room and for two days had had a grand old time, buying people drinks and generally celebrating. On the third day, when Joe had opened up, he had found Amos lying on the boardwalk, frozen to death. 'He'd even crossed his arms across his chest,' Joe told him. 'We gave him a nice funeral.' Joe could see that Zachary was visibly upset, 'Here's the letter,' he said softly.

'Read it, please.'

Joe read, *Zachary. had a good wake, wish you had been here. Don't have much of value, sure did like this rifle though. It's a Ferguson, only about a hundred of them ever made. I took it off a British officer in the war of 1814. The pistols are Parkers, good weapons. Time sure runs away. Seems like only yesterday that we fought the British. That's when I should have died, young, and in battle, instead of hanging on this long. Near as I can figure, I'm 86. Don't get me wrong, I had a high old time. Don't know many people got to be my age, though. I had me a squaw back in about 1820; her name was Sings Sweetly. Sure did love that girl. We had us a baby boy, at our wintering place on the Colorado River. The boy died after two days and Sweet followed a few days later. Perhaps me and Sweet will meet up in the spirit world and go roaming again.*

Don't get upset over what I've done, I've seen plenty of men froze to death, never looked like it hurt much. Wish you'd come by fifty years ago, son, we'd have had a fine old time. Like to think that my boy would have been like you. Hope you put one into Lou for me.

Amos
PS. No change from that fifty dollars.

'Silly old bastard,' Zachary said. 'Think I'll lie down for a while.' He stood and picked up his things, 'By the way, you'll hear this on the wind so I'll tell you now: Clare and I got married in Butte.'

Joe was at a loss. 'Well, congratulations. Look, Zachary, we haven't known each other long, but I reckon we're friends. Do you want to talk about anything?'

Zachary gave him a sad smile. 'No, Joe, but thanks.'

Chapter Six

Over the ensuing weeks, Zachary saw Clare several times. It was a month to the day of their marriage when Clare appeared and told him she wasn't pregnant.

'How do you feel?' Zachary asked.

'I don't know, to be truthful, I've spent all this time telling myself everything would work out. Now, I feel relieved I suppose.' Zachary thought that this was a strange answer.

They fell into a pattern. Zachary visited Top Hat when he could, and Clare visited him whenever she was in town. They met at the church dances. Clare was regaining her confidence slowly, and Zachary was hard-pressed to get a dance.

At the beginning of December, a marshal and deputy arrived in Deer Creek. The deputy, James Shockley, was the grandson of an old lawman named Arnold Blight, whom Zachary knew quite well.

The Saturday before Christmas Day, the weather was milder although snow still threatened. Zachary decided to go out to Top Hat with Christmas presents, in an attempt to rekindle Clare's interest in him. He hired a buggy for the trip. He had to detour to the farming community, and arrived at Top Hat about 8 p.m. It was obvious that the family was entertaining.

Steven English answered his knock on the door. 'You don't have to knock, Zachary, come in,' he said.

Zachary was embarrassed. 'I'm sorry, I didn't know you had visitors.'

Steven took some of the parcels and they headed for the office. Sounds of music and laughter wafted down the hallway. Now it was Steven's turn to be embarrassed. 'We're having a Christmas party for the hands and some friends. Didn't Clare invite you?'

'She probably left a message, but I didn't get it. Happens a lot,' Zachary replied. Both men knew he was lying.

Zachary had two rather large parcels for Clare and her mother. He had bought them both sheepskin overcoats. To Steven, he gave Amos Allnut's rifle, pistols and accessories.

'I can't take them, Zachary, he left them to you.'

'What good's a flintlock rifle to a one-armed man, Steven?'

Steven caressed the old rifle lovingly, 'When I was a boy, old Amos used to win all the turkey shoots with this gun. I'll tell you what, I'll keep it all here for you.' Zachary smiled. 'Well, come join the party,' Steven said.

'No thanks, I'd better go. Looks like snow again. I don't want to embarrass Clare.'

Steven wanted Zachary to stay but he refused, so he accompanied him out to the buggy. 'I'm sorry, Zachary,' he said.

'Oh well, it was worth a try. See you,' Zachary said, as he reined the horse around and drove out of the yard.

In the large dining-room, people were dancing. Clare was dancing and laughing with Quentin Quirk.

'I want a word, Clare,' Steven said.

'In a minute, Daddy,' she replied.

Steven grabbed her by the arm, 'Now,' he said sternly.

She followed her father to his office. 'Isn't this a grand party?' she asked. 'Now, what's the matter, Mr Grumpy?' She spotted the parcels. 'What's all this?' she enquired.

'Did you invite Zachary tonight?' her father asked.

Clare blanched noticeably. 'No, I. . . .'

Her father exploded. 'No! Good God, Clare, he's your husband!'

'In name only, Father.'

'In name only, what the hell does that mean? You're a married woman, Clare, and that carries responsibilities. You're out there dancing with that clown, Quentin, and at the dances you flirt with anything in pants. You're behaving like some cheap saloon girl!' her father yelled.

'Zachary married me to solve my problem, Father,' Clare ventured.

'He married you because he loves you! I think he hoped that you might grow to feel the same about him, once you got over the shock of what happened.'

Clare was stunned. 'I'm sorry, Father, I didn't know,' she said softly. 'What should I do?'

'About Zachary? I'm damned if I know. Other than that, start behaving like the lady I expect you to be.' Steven picked up one of the parcels and threw it at her. 'There, Zachary brought you a Christmas present, then he left. Didn't want to embarrass you. You've got some serious thinking to do, girl,' her father said, then walked out and left her.

Clare was shocked by her conversation with her father; he was right, she had to think. She tried on her coat; it felt wonderful. She and her mother had looked at them in a catalogue at the store. Zachary must have ordered them quite some time ago. She walked out on to the porch. The night was cold and crisp, just how she loved it. 'Marvellous night, isn't it?' she heard Quentin say from behind her. She nodded.

'We're staying overnight,' he continued.

'I know.'

'How about when everyone's asleep, I come to your room.'

'I beg your pardon?' Clare asked in disbelief.

'You heard.'

'How dare you, Quentin. I'm married; what kind of a person do you think I am?'

'You're a married woman who doesn't get on with her husband, everyone knows that. He's not even here. But married women have needs, and I'm just the boy to fix that for you.'

Clare spun around and slapped him, 'If I have needs, Quentin, believe me, you would be the last person on earth I'd come to.'

'You bitch!' Quentin yelled,and raised his hand to her.

In the shadows, someone cocked a gun. 'Do it, you die,' they heard Sam Lockwood say.

At breakfast, two days before Christmas, Clare rather sheepishly asked if she could go to town and ask Zachary to spend Christmas with them. Steven, who had been fairly short with her since the party, said, 'Yes; take two men with you.'

The new marshal was now using a room at the livery stable as an office. Clare went there and asked Deputy Shockley where she would find Marshal Concannon. 'He's gone,' Shockley replied.

Clare stared. 'Gone? Where?'

'He left for Canada, yesterday.'

Clare just stood, shocked beyond belief.

'Listen,' Shockley said, 'how about stayin' in town and havin' supper with me?'

'I'm a married woman, Deputy,' Clare said abstractedly.

The deputy laughed. 'So what? Everyone knows you've been puttin' yourself about. Why did you marry half a man?'

Clare blushed profusely, partly from shame and partly in anger. 'Deputy, I wouldn't go to supper with you if it was the last chance I'd ever get to have a meal. As for Zachary, if he's half a man, how come they still had to send two of you to replace him?'

As she stormed out, Clare met the marshal coming in. 'Your deputy has a poor attitude, Marshal,' she told him. 'He's undermining all the good work my husband did here.'

The marshal watched her go. 'Bitch,' his deputy said.

The marshal swung on him angrily. 'She's right, I've had other complaints about how you speak to women. You're fired.'

'You can't!'

'I just did, son. Badge please.'

Clare rushed to the saloon and found Joe Malone. She asked to talk to him and he took her to his office. 'That deputy said Zachary's gone to Canada, is that right?' she asked.

'Yes, yesterday morning. He got a letter from Virginia, said it was from his brother. He sat by the fire and read it over and over, for about an hour. Then he asked if I had a map of Canada. He wanted a place called Chatham, which is in Ontario. The easiest way to get there, is to go to Michigan, then cross into Canada below Lake Saint Clare. Next morning, he was here paying his bill; then he left.' Clare turned away so that Joe wouldn't see the tears in her eyes. 'I tried to get him to stay, Clare,' Joe said gently. 'Wanted him to spend Christmas with us at least. He said, "Christmas is just another day, Joe". I asked was he going to see you and he said, "No point flogging a dead horse", then he left. I'm sorry.'

Clare ran from the office and out of the saloon.

Zachary crossed into Canada from Detroit, after a journey of over 2,000 miles. By the time he reached Chatham, it was mid-February. He looked for a marshal, but found a Royal Canadian Mounted Policeman. After introducing himself, he told the Mountie he was looking for a brother and sister, named Benjamin and Josephine, who had come here before the war.

'Slaves?' the man enquired. 'You can't take 'em back, you know.'

'Believe me, nothing is further from my mind. Do you know them by any chance?'

The Mountie, who looked to be part Indian, studied Zachary for a time. Eventually he said, 'Yes, I know them. They're respected members of our community, as are many other ex-slaves. If you do them harm, I'll be on you like locusts on a corn crop.'

'Fair enough,' Zachary replied.

Zachary followed the directions. It was a fine day, even if it was still a bit cold. He rode into a neat farmyard and immediately he knew that his search was over. A man stood holding a young mule. His wife, a light-skinned black woman with close-cropped curly hair, stood half-hidden behind him, with two children. She was holding a hoe. The man took it from his wife.

Zachary smiled slightly. 'Mr Le Clerc?' he asked.

'Yes,' the man answered.

'I mean you no harm, sir,' Zachary said.

The man relaxed. 'What can I do for you?'

'If I may, I would like to speak to your wife.'

Jean Le Clerc looked at his wife, who nodded slightly. 'Very well, sir,' he said.

Zachary dismounted, years of searching took their toll and a tear rolled down his cheek. 'Hello, Jos,' he said.

The woman put her hands to her face and screamed, 'Zachary?'

'What's left, my love,' Zachary replied.

Jos looked from Zachary to her husband, 'Go on, girl,' her husband said gently.

Jos moved, hesitantly at first, then she ran and threw herself into Zachary's arms. They held each other for minutes, then Jos took his hand and led him to where her family stood. She introduced her husband as John, her children, Annette and Zachary. The children hid behind their father's legs. 'Ben will be here soon,' Jos said excitedly.

No sooner had she said it, than a wagon drove into the yard. Zachary knew Ben, instantly. On the wagon also, was a woman nursing a baby. Jos grabbed Zachary by the hand and dragged him towards the wagon. 'Ben, look who's here,' she cried.

It didn't take Ben long to realize who it was. 'Well, well, Massa Zachary, you can't take us back, you know.'

'I've no intention of trying to do that, Ben. I just wanted to know that you're both well, that's all.'

'Oh, we're fine, massa. You people sold us, you bastards.'

Jos tried to intervene but Ben wouldn't be put off. He glared hatefully at Zachary. 'If you weren't a cripple, I'd beat you to death,' he declared forcefully.

Zachary felt defeated. 'I understand how you feel, Ben. I don't want to disrupt your lives.' He turned to his horse, 'I have a letter here from your mother. Read it, then if you want me to leave, I'll leave.' Zachary handed Ben the letter from Tilly, that Artemus had sent. Ben and Jos took it almost reverently.

It was half an hour before Ben and Jos reappeared. They had both been crying. Jos carried the letter and passed it to her husband. Ben stood with his hands on his wife's shoulders and just looked at Zachary. 'So, we're half-brothers.'

'Yes,' Zachary replied.

'He still sold us.'

'Yes, and it was my fault. I've searched for you for fifteen years to say I'm sorry.'

'Why is it your fault?' Ben asked.

'Because I told Father that I was going to marry Jos. Then he sent me to Kentucky and sold you.'

Both men stared at each other. To break the impasse, Zachary opened his saddle-bags. 'I have a present for each of you. I bought them in Kentucky. I've carried them with me for fifteen years.' He removed a small parcel. 'Jos, you always liked those linen bonnets that my sisters wore. I've kept it as nice as I could, had to wash the starch out of it, though.'

Jos unwrapped the parcel and shook out the bonnet.

'Sorry about the stain on the ribbon,' Zachary said, 'It's blood. I was carrying my saddle-bags when my arm was blown off.'

Jos tried the bonnet on and, even unstarched, it suited her well. She kissed Zachary on the cheek, 'Thank you,' she said.

Zachary turned to Ben. 'You always wanted a Bowie knife, Ben. I had it engraved.'

Ben unwrapped the knife and stared at it for quite some time. Then he read the inscription: 'To Ben, my best friend.'

Ben embraced Zachary. 'I'm sorry, Zachary,' he said.

'Don't worry about it,' Zachary told him, as he wiped his eyes. Even his blind eye still shed tears. 'I have something else for you, too.' He removed his wallet and handed both Ben and Jos a large sum of money. 'Father got two thousand five hundred dollars for both of you. I own Truro now, and I refuse to profit from the sale of human beings, especially those who are the best friends I ever had. It won't make up for what happened, but I can do no more.'

Zachary stayed with his friends for two weeks. They had taken the name of Martin, the woman to whom they had been sold. When she had discovered that she was dying, she had given Ben and Jos their freedom. However, she was afraid that her son, who was a terrible lecher, wouldn't honour her wishes, especially where Jos was concerned, so she had got them into the underground railroad. Things were going well for them, and would be even better now with the money Zachary had given them.

Ben and Jos wanted Zachary to stay in Canada, perhaps buy some land, but he declined. 'This is your life, not mine. Besides, how many one-armed farmers do you know?'

After emotional goodbyes and promises to write, Zachary rode out, headed for Virginia, one of his life's ambitions realized.

Chapter Seven

Zachary spent a short time at Truro. He arranged for Tilly and Cyrus, and his brother Artemus and his wife, to travel to Canada to be reunited with Tilly's children.

Whilst in Richmond, Zachary accepted the job as marshal of an oil town called Pioneer Run, in Pennsylvania. This area had originally been a farming community. Now it was a boom town, with more than its share of lawless individuals. His contract was for $1,000 a month and half the fines he collected.

It was early spring when he arrived in Pioneer Run. The outskirts of the town now held an unruly collection of shacks and oil wells, lumber and pipes. A mess. He saw a sign on a big tent, that read, 'Jennie's Kitchen', and smiled to himself.

Zachary reined in at the general store owned by Robert Hall, the mayor. He introduced himself and the mayor stole a furtive glance at his sleeve.

'You come well recommended,' he said.

'So do I stay, or go?' Zachary asked.

'You stay, of course. It was just a shock; I didn't know about your arm. I'm sorry if I made you feel uncomfortable.'

There was a commotion on the boardwalk. Two young men were harassing two women holding shopping baskets. One of the women was crying. 'This is just one of our problems,' the mayor said. 'Women aren't safe on the streets.'

Zachary asked for his badge and an axe handle, then he stepped out on to the boardwalk. He drove the axe handle into the stomach of one of the young men. The other reached for a pistol he had stuck in his belt. Zachary hit him on the wrist and he screamed.

'Pick up these ladies' groceries,' Zachary told them. 'Now, out into the street and lean on the hitch rail.' They did so. Zachary hit them both a resounding blow on the rump. 'Now you listen to me,' Zachary said. 'I'm the new marshal. I won't stand for this kind of behaviour, is that clear?'

'Yes, sir,' the two men answered.

'Good. Now, you'll carry these two ladies' baskets home.' Zachary put the axe handle under the stump of his arm and removed his hat. 'May I say you ladies look fresher then flowers on a spring morning.' The ladies left, giggling.

'Well now, Mayor,' Zachary said. 'I might as well get straight to work. Where do all the rowdies congregate?'

The mayor took Zachary to a large tent that was a makeshift saloon. Zachary walked in and struck the bar with the flat side of his axe handle. There was an immediate silence. 'My name is Zachary Concannon,' he told the gathering. 'I'm the new marshal of Pioneer Run and the surrounding oilfield. I have only one rule, and that is, everyone behaves himself. I don't mind a bit of high spirits, but I won't tolerate unruly behaviour.'

At a table, four men had been playing cards. One spoke. 'We ran the last three lawmen out, we'll get rid o' you, too.'

Zachary moved to the table. The man who had spoken was one of the biggest men he had ever seen. 'Let me guess,' Zachary said, 'they call you Moose.'

'Yeah,' the man answered. 'How'd you know?'

'Well, I saw a moose just recently; he certainly was big and strong, but he sure looked stupid. As I said, it was a guess.'

The man glared at Zachary. Another man at the table with Moose, stood; he wore a six-gun tied down on the right.

'And you're the local fast gun, I suppose,' Zachary commented.

'That's right, Marshal, and what do we call you? One Eye? Or One Arm?' Everyone laughed.

'No, no, gunfighter, you can call me Marshal. How about you show me how fast and dangerous you are.'

The man went for his gun. Before he had it halfway out, Zachary hit him in the face with his axe handle. The man dropped his gun and grabbed his face. 'Shit! You broke my nose, you bastard!' the man screamed.

'Don't worry, gunfighter, you'll recover. You won't recover from being dead though, remember that.'

Zachary turned his attention to the rest of the crowd. 'Right, now that I've met all the town's characters, there's one thing more I must tell you: from now on, no one brings a gun into town. You'll deposit them at the livery at the south end of town, and . . . what's at the north end?' he asked the mayor.

'Blacksmith,' the astounded mayor answered.

'The blacksmith at the north end. Fee is ten cents. If you bring your gun into town the fine is twenty dollars and you forfeit the weapon. So I suggest you leave them home. If anyone needs to be shot, believe me, I'm more than capable of doing it.'

The drinkers watched the two men depart. 'What do we do, Moose?' someone asked.

'Give him a few weeks to settle in, and then we'll run him off, that's what we'll do,' Moose replied. Everyone agreed.

On the street, the mayor looked at Zachary and laughed nervously. 'You're staying at Ryan's Saloon,' he said.

'Right. I'll settle in, then I'm going to Jennie's for a meal.'

*

Clare had returned home in a high state of agitation. To realize what people thought of her, distressed her. To know that Zachary had gone off without saying anything to her, was even more upsetting. She knew why he would have gone to Canada, looking for Ben and Jos, but was upset at his not telling her. He should have, even if they were just friends, but she was his wife, whatever the reason. How hurt he must have been to do that. Too late, she realized that she had feelings for this enigmatic man, strong feelings. Christmas was a subdued time for the English family. Clare knew that for her father to be critical of her, she had behaved badly. Her first priority was to repair their relationship. She had composed a speech, and, with resolve, had approached her father as he sat in the parlour. She stood before him, but words wouldn't come, only tears.

Steven reached out and drew his daughter on to his lap and rocked her as she cried. 'Ah, baby,' he said into her hair.

'What should I do, Daddy?' she asked eventually.

'What do you want to do, baby?' her father replied.

'I want to see Zachary. I want to talk to him. I – I don't know, I took him for granted. Deep down I never thought that he'd leave. I don't know why I acted like I did. It's like as if being a married woman gave me a sense of freedom, and I could behave as I liked. I was a married woman without any responsibilties to the marriage. All I did was embarrass you and make myself look like a tramp. I'm not like that, Daddy.'

'I know, darling, I know.'

'I'd like to go and find Zachary, Daddy.'

'You can't go trudging all over Canada, Clare.'

'I know. With this snow, I wouldn't be able to go anywhere until the spring, anyway. I think I should go to Richmond and see Zachary's brother. They seem to keep in touch.'

'I don't want you going alone, and your mother and I can't go.' At that moment, there was a knock on the door. 'Oh, sorry,' Sam Lockwood said. 'I'll come back later.'

'No, no, Sam, come in please,' Steven said. 'Clare wants to go to Virginia in the spring, would you go with her?'

Sam looked nervously from one to the other. 'I can't go anywhere near Missouri, Steven, you know that.'

'You hear that, Clare? You're not to go anywhere near Missouri,' Steven told his daughter.

After waiting impatiently for the snow to clear away, Clare and Sam arrived in Richmond at the beginning of March. To find directions to Truro, they went to the marshal's office. The marshal eyed them speculatively. 'Can I give you some advice, young lady?' he asked.

'You can give it, Marshal, I might not take it.'

The dour marshal gave her a brief smile, 'Fair enough,' he said. 'Well, here it is. Many a carpet-bagger and profiteer has tried to take Truro from the Concannons. That Artemus is as sharp as a whip, but he's a frail-looking young fella. Then there's Zachary, a whole different kettle o' fish. Zachary actually owns Truro, and he don't stand for anyone interfering with his people. He comes riding, people have a habit of dying. So, if you're thinking that a woman can succeed where men can't, I suggest that you turn around and get back on the train, and take your pet gunfighter with you.'

Clare smiled. 'Thank you, Marshal. I assure you that I mean the Concannons no harm. As for my pet gunfighter, Sam is my uncle and my travelling companion. Now, will you direct us? Or should I ask someone else.'

'You don't need directions. I saw Artemus and Cyrus pass by not ten minutes ago. I reckon you'll find them at the livery stable, looking at some heavy horses that just came in. You can't miss 'em. Artemus is slight built and fair, Cyrus is as black as night and big as a house.'

'Thank you, Marshal,' Clare said and they left.

At the livery stable, several men were leaning on the yard rails looking at the horses. That was until Clare arrived, then they looked at her with a fair degree of enthusiasm, until the spectre of Sam loomed alongside. It was easy to pick out

Artemus and Cyrus. The marshal was right: Cyrus was a giant. He must have been three or four inches taller than Zachary, and as hard as a rock, despite the encroachment of grey hair.

Clare touched the slightly built Artemus on the shoulder. 'Mr Concannon?' she asked nervously.

Artemus turned, he was about 5'9" tall and had the facial features of his brother. He was fair and quite pale. He would have been a sickly child, Clare concluded. 'Yes, ma'am?' he asked in a voice similar to Zachary's.

'I'm Clare, Clare Concannon.'

'I'm afraid that means nothing to me, ma'am. Are you saying you're some distant relative? Father was an only child; we have no paternal relatives that we know of.'

Clare felt her eyes sting. Zachary hadn't told his brother that he was married. 'Artemus, I'm Zachary's wife.'

Both Artemus and Cyrus looked at her, stunned. 'You must be Cyrus,' Clare said, offering her hand. 'Did Zachary find Ben and Jos in Canada?'

'Yes, ma'am, he did,' Cyrus replied in a rumbling voice.

After an embarrassing silence, Artemus insisted that she and Sam stay with him and his wife. Clare agreed, reluctantly.

Cyrus drove the wagon and Artemus gave them a guided tour. They stopped at a huge set of gates, 'The old mansion house,' Artemus told them.

Clare took it all in. The huge house with its large portico and pillars, manicured gardens with just the first hint of colour in the flower beds and trees. 'It's magnificent,' Clare said. 'I bet you're sad you lost it.'

'Me personally, no,' Artemus told her. 'Besides, it was lose that or lose everything. Zachary had to raise money quickly or be saddled with a crushing debt. I think that from Zack's point of view, it was poetic justice. He took from our parents what they loved the most, like they had done to him when father sold Ben and Jos. Apart from that, we couldn't have maintained it after the war. It took twenty servants to run that house and the gardens. Couldn't afford it, simple.'

Two young men galloped up on fine blood horses. 'Sons of the owner,' Artemus told them.

'Hello Art,' one said, fighting his horse. 'Bought a couple of slaves, have you? Like the girl; how about selling her to me?'

Sam made to stand up, but Clare stilled him, interested to see how Artemus would handle these loud mouths, who now sat, leering at her.

'My name is Artemus, you loud-mouthed bastard,' Artemus said. 'As for the young lady, she is Zachary's wife. You remember Zachary, he's the one with the gun. The one who gave the both of you a thrashing. A one-armed man who beat the shit out of you both. So, go ahead, insult his wife, I'll tell him next time I write. Won't be long before you see old Buck on the road.'

The two young men blanched visibly, 'I'm sorry, ma'am, sorry Artemus,' said the one who had done the talking.

'Sorry just about says it,' Artemus replied. 'And don't gallop your horses on our land, I've told you that before.'

'No, sir.' The young men turned away.

'You watch out for that big ol' bay horse now, won't you?'

Cyrus laughed, a deep rumbling sound like thunder.

Clare was greeted warmly if warily, by Sarah, Artemus's wife. The wariness was short lived and they were soon good friends. Clare was introduced to Zachary's parents, his sisters and their husbands. The sisters especially, seemed antagonistic towards Zachary. Clare got the feeling that they blamed Zachary for their diminished station in life. The parents hardly acknowledged her at all. They were bitter about their fall from grace. At one point, Clare got so fed up with their attacks on Zachary, that she had to respond.

'Don't you think that things were hard for Zachary? Do you think that it was easy for him to declare for the Union? Do you think it's easy for him now, with his injuries? Having to work hard at a dangerous job, to keep you all living here? Then he has to listen to you moan all the time. The way of life you long for is gone, get used to it.'

'Don't preach to us,' sister Mary said indignantly. 'Who do you think you are? The new lady of the manor?'

'I'm Zachary's wife, and we have no intention of settling here and listening to you complain for the rest of your life.'

Artemus grinned at Clare and winked.

The revelation was Tilly. Clare was drawn to her immediately. Zachary was right, she was a regal-looking woman. She, Cyrus and Artemus and family, had only just returned from visiting Ben and Jos for two weeks. Tilly had lost all contact with her children after they had been sold. They had all journeyed to New York State, and had met Ben, Jos and their families at Niagara Falls, for an emotional reunion.

Clare braced herself and told her new-found friends what had happened to her and what had happened between herself and Zachary. As the tears began to flow, Tilly held her gently.

Artemus informed her that Zachary was now the marshal of Pioneer Run, in Pennsylvania. This was her destination, Clare decided. On their way to the station, Clare asked Cyrus to stop at O'Connell's Emporium. It was easy for Clare to pick out Alice.

'You must be Alice,' Clare said.

'Yes, Alice White. Do I know you?'

Clare smiled. 'No, but I feel that I know you. I'm Clare Concannon, Zachary's wife; he told me all about you.'

Alice blushed. 'All?' she enquired.

'Yes, all. But he didn't demean you in any way. In fact, he admires you greatly. He told me about the two of you, because at the time I had just had a terrible experience, and, for some reason, I needed to know intimate details of his life. He told me about you with the greatest respect. He said that during the war, the thought of you kept him warm on many a cold night. He also said that when he met you again after the war, he was impressed by your dignity. That helped me overcome what had happened to me, so, thank you.'

Alice hugged her. 'I'm glad he told you then, Clare. You should have known him before the war God, he was a beautiful boy. To see him now, a lonely, bitter man, well, it breaks my heart. How are things between you and him?'

'Why do you ask?'

'I sense things.'

'Not good,' Clare had to admit. 'But I want to make things right. I've realized that I love Zachary very much.'

'Then you'll make things right, Clare, I know it.'

It was the first day of spring when Clare and Sam arrived in Pioneer Run. They hired a wagon to take them to the marshal's office. Here, they were informed by a slightly inebriated occupant, that the marshal had been called to a disturbance at the big tent, that served as a saloon. They headed there.

Through a sea of pain and nausea, Zachary had to admit that this Moose could really hit. He was being firmly held by two men, and Moose hit him again, a left and right to the ribs.

'Let him go!' he heard someone scream above the cheers of the onlookers. He looked to his left. If he hadn't known better, he'd have sworn it was Clare. She was holding a revolver.

'You won't shoot me, darlin',' Moose replied.

Someone Zachary could have sworn was Sam Lockwood stepped up, also holding a gun, 'If she doesn't, I will,' he said.

The two men let Zachary go and he collapsed to the ground. The woman hurried to him and knelt. It was Clare.

'Get my eyepatch, please,' he asked.

'Don't worry about that,' Clare replied.

'Get my damned eyepatch, please!' Zachary yelled at her.

Moose was wearing it. Clare snatched it from him and gave it to Zachary who put it on. 'What the hell are you doing here?' Zachary asked. 'Run out of men to flirt with in Montana?'

Clare ignored this remark. 'You're my husband, Zachary, where else should I be?'

Zachary laughed; it ended in a fit of coughing. 'I'm not your husband, Clare, I'm just the man whose name you use.'

'Let me help you up.'

'No, leave me alone. Go to hell.'

Clare moved to where Sam stood, covering

everyone with his gun. She watched as, with great difficulty, Zachary hauled himself to his feet.

'Right,' Zachary said, 'You've had your fun, now it's pay-up time.' He demanded the men's wallets and took all their money. 'That will have to do,' he told them.

'You can't take it all,' one of the men protested.

'I can fine you as much as I like,' Zachary replied. He moved on to where Moose stood. 'Well, Mr Moose, you can really hit, I'll give you that. Think you can do it when no one's holding me?' Moose grinned evilly and headed for the street.

When Moose turned, Zachary kicked him between the legs. As he doubled over, Moose met Zachary's knee on the way up. It hit him right in the face and he fell to the ground. He was tough though, and tried to rise. Zachary hit him with an uppercut that sent him over backwards and he lay still.

Zachary turned to the stunned crowd, 'Anyone else?' he asked. No one answered. Zachary smiled briefly. 'You're pathetic,' he said to the crowd, 'I'm embarrassed to say that I enforce the law here. The money I'm getting paid, I ought to arrest myself for highway robbery. Now get this trash off the street. Before you go, there's one more thing: this young lady you're all drooling over, is my wife, Clare. There's only one thing you need to know about her: touch her, you die.'

Zachary turned to Sam, 'Ryan's Saloon,' he said, 'I'll see you there in twenty minutes.' Then he walked away to his office and put the money in the safe. He let Lester, the town drunk, out of the cell and gave him a dollar. 'You eat, don't drink, that clear?'

'Yes, Zachary.'

'Go to Jennie's, please, and ask her to bring her bag of tricks to my room, in about half an hour.'

'Yes, Zachary.'

'After you've had your meal, get a bath and come back here to sleep, all right?'

'Yes, Zachary.'

Zachary went to the saloon. 'Upstairs,' the barman told him.

Sam was in Zachary's room. 'Down the hall,' he said.

Zachary found Clare and David Ryan inspecting a small suite. 'The Presidential suite,' David told him proudly. The suite consisted of a bedroom and a parlour. Off the side of the bedroom, there was a small bathroom. 'Look at this,' David Ryan told him excitedly. The bathroom had its own water heater, that was connected to a water tank up the hill. 'All you do is start the fire and turn this tap on, then it heats water as long as you keep the fire going. It's the latest thing. I've never let these rooms before. Perhaps I'll rename it the Honeymoon Suite.'

'Light it up, please,' Zachary asked, then showed him out.

Clare waited while Zachary just looked at her. 'What side of the bed do you want?' she asked nervously.

'Don't be ridiculous,' he replied. 'Why are you here, Clare? Do I have to sign divorce papers or something?'

'Zachary, I don't want to divorce you. I think we could have a good life together.'

'Well, we can't. We had an agreement and you'll live up to it. If you don't I'll divorce you.'

'On what grounds?'

'How about non-consummation of our marriage?'

Clare blushed profusely. 'I'll deny that, Zachary. Even though it would be terribly embarrassing, I'll have myself examined by a doctor. He could tell I'm not a virgin.'

'Good, do that. I'll bring Quentin and a train load of those farm boys from Montana. They'll all testify that you behave like some two-bit whore. And when I swear on the Bible that I've never touched you, they'll all be as interested as hell to know who got you into bed.'

Clare hung her head in shame and embarrassment.

'I'll not embarrass you while you're here, Clare, but I want you out of my life. Now, if you don't mind, I'll have a bath.'

As Clare sat in the parlour, someone knocked on the door. Clare answered and found a plumpish woman and a very well-dressed man standing there. 'I'm Jenny, this is Max. Is Zachary here?' the woman asked. Clare stepped aside and let them enter.

Zachary emerged from the bedroom. He

thanked Jenny for coming, then removed his shirt, it was the first time Clare had seen his arm. It had been taken off just above the elbow.

'You'll be stiff tomorrow,' Jenny said, as she applied liniment to Zachary's ribs, then bound him up with a bandage. 'That's all I can do for you,' she said. 'Try to rest.'

'Anything I can do, Zachary?' the man asked. 'No thanks, Max,' Zachary replied.

'I'm Clare, Zachary's wife,' Clare blurted out, when it was obvious that Zachary wasn't going to introduce her.

After an awkward silence, the visitors left. Zachary finished dressing and, with great difficulty, strapped on his gun. 'You can't go out, Zachary, you need to rest,' Clare said.

'Go home, Clare,' was all he said; then he left.

Zachary went to his former room to see Sam. 'Why the hell are you here?' he demanded.

'Clare wanted to see you and I'm here as her bodyguard.'

'How did you find me?'

'We went to Virginia and saw your brother. We had a nice time. Clare got on real well with Artemus.'

'Not with my parents and sisters though,' Zachary said with a wry smile.

'No, but that's because they dislike you, not her.'

'Probably,' Zachary replied. 'Look, I have a rule: no one carries a gun in town, not even you. So come to the jail, I have lots of guns. Pick one you can carry in your boot and stay close to Clare; there are some unsavoury types in this town.'

'Thanks,' Sam replied.

Zachary turned to leave then stopped. 'Incidentally,' he said, 'when I first got here, I was going through some old fliers. There was one about twenty-five years old, for someone with the same name as you. He was wanted in Missouri for bank robbery. Must have been a wild old bastard. I wrote to the authorities there and told them I'd seen this old coot shot dead in Kansas last year.' Zachary paused at the door, 'Don't do anything to make me say I was wrong; and make Clare go home.'

'Thanks, Zachary. As for Clare, well, she's determined to stay until she can talk to you,' but Zachary left.

Clare waited for Zachary until midnight, then tiredness overtook her and she retired. She woke at about 6.30 a.m., and found Zachary asleep on the couch in the parlour. When she entered, he awoke instantly. He tried to sit up but he couldn't, so he rolled off the couch into a kneeling position, then stood. He looked ill and was obviously in great pain. 'You still here?' he asked, then he went and started the water heater.

Clare dressed while Zachary was in the bath. There was a knock on the door; it was Jenny again. She left more liniment for Zachary to rub on his ribs. Zachary came into the parlour carrying his shirt. Clare's heart raced. He was strongly built, except for the stump of his arm, which seemed to be a bit withered. The sabre cut that ran down his face, carried on down over his right breast. He'd certainly had more than his share of injuries.

'Jenny left this,' Clare said, passing over the lotion. 'She your lady friend?'

'She's a friend, OK?'

'I just wanted to know.'

'My friends are none of your business. But no, she's not my lady friend. She's married to Max, the man who was with her. I knew him in the cavalry. They're boomers – they follow the boom towns. She has her kitchen; Max is a gambler. They are good people and probably the richest people I know, your parents included. Jenny is a marvellous nurse.'

Zachary rubbed the liniment on his ribs, which were now quite discoloured. Clare offered to help but was firmly rebuffed. As upset as she was at not being able to help, Clare was intrigued to see a one-armed man do for himself. To rebandage his ribs, Zachary tied the bandage to a hat hook on the door. He held the end against his chest; then, turning in circles, slowly wound the bandage on, pausing now and then to adjust it. The only trouble he had, was, after taking the bandage off the door, picking up the tape to tie it off. Clare handed him the tape that hung down his back. 'Thank you,' he said, grudgingly.

Zachary finished dressing. He had trouble putting on his socks and he had to sit on the bed to buckle on his gunbelt and tie it to his leg. It seemed so terribly sad to Clare, but she didn't offer to help.

'You want breakfast?' Zachary asked.

'Yes, please,' Clare answered ecstatically; this was a start. They collected Sam and had breakfast in the saloon. They were served by Margaret Ryan, the owner's wife, who positively beamed at Clare.

'I'm so glad to meet you,' she said. 'Your husband has made such a difference to our town. Mind you, there are going to be some very upset young ladies, when they find out he's married, goodness me, yes.'

Zachary glared at her. 'Leave any time, Margaret,' he said. Margaret left, laughing.

Clare asked if she could ride Buck, if she and Sam took a look around.

'Make sure there's a horse for me, then, please,' Zachary replied as he stood to leave.

'What time will I see you for dinner?' Clare asked.

Zachary glared. 'Don't wait up, dear,' he said facetiously.

Chapter Eight

For three days Clare and Sam explored Pioneer Run. The excitement and chaos of the place proved infectious. Clare spoke to many of the men who had oil wells who were only to happy to share their knowledge and experiences with the woman who was already being referred to as The Lady Clare.

As for Zachary, he came and went as he pleased. Clare never saw him in the evenings, and once he never came home at all. Worried, she and Sam hurried to the jail before breakfast. Lester the drunk told her that Zachary had been out until 3 a.m. and had slept in one of the cells.

'Does he do this often?' Clare enquired.

'Oh yes, ma'am, quite often. But don't worry, I watch over him. Zachary is my friend, probably my only friend.'

'Why are you here, Lester?' Clare asked.

'I'm under arrest, ma'am. I must stay in jail and sober until I pay off my gambling debt to Zachary.'

Clare smiled. 'But you're not locked up. You could leave.'

Lester straightened himself up and said with dignity, 'I'm an honorable man, ma'am. I used to be a schoolteacher. My honour is all I have left.'

'I can see that you're a gentleman, Lester, and I apologize if I intimated anything else. How much do you owe Zachary?'

'Three hundred and forty thousand dollars, ma'am.'

Clare burst out laughing. 'You'll be here forever.'

The old man smiled a soft smile. 'Oh no, ma'am. Zachary allows me to work it off. I get ten dollars a day, a huge sum for a janitor, but he agreed to it, so I don't complain.'

Again Clare laughed; she enjoyed talking to this man, who wasn't quite as old as she had first thought. 'You do a good job, I must admit that.'

'Thank you. It also allows Zachary to get some sleep, without having to keep his eye open. We've asked the town council for deputies, but they haven't arrived as yet.'

Before Clare could continue, Zachary came from the cells. Lester hurriedly got him a pitcher of water and a towel so he could wash. 'You eaten yet?' Zachary asked the old man.

'No, sir, I've been on watch while you slept.'

Zachary looked at Lester with obvious affection, 'Well, if you're looking for a raise, you're out of luck. What I pay you is outrageous.'

Clare could see that the older man really enjoyed this banter. 'A workman is worthy of his hire, sir,' he replied. 'Besides, I think you cheat at cards.'

'I don't need to cheat,' Zachary replied. 'Because you are without doubt the worst poker player I've ever met. Now, come on, we'll go to Jennie's for breakfast. If you're good I'll buy you flapjacks and maple syrup; if you misbehave, you just get to watch me eat mine.'

Lester offered his arm to Clare and they set off. At the door she looked back and caught Zachary smiling. This was good.

Clare rarely saw Zachary for dinner. A few days later, she made a point of going to Jennie's later than normal, determined to dine with him. He came in about nine. Clare saw Jenny hurry to him and point out where she was sitting in the still crowded tent.

'Where's Sam?' Zachary asked by way of greeting.

'He's playing poker. Don't worry, he can see me.'

'What do you want, Clare?' Zachary asked as he sat.

'I want to have dinner with my husband and I want to talk.'

Jenny came and they both ordered roast beef. 'What do you want to talk about?' Zachary asked when they were alone.

'Well, Sam and I have been looking around, and

I think this whole oil thing is terribly exciting. There are these two brothers who each own a partly drilled well. They've run out of money, and the driller, who is that Moose person by the way, won't drill any more unless he gets paid.' She paused.

'So?' Zachary asked.

'So I'd like to buy their wells. I've spoken to them and they've given me until tomorrow to decide.'

'How much?'

'Five thousand dollars each,' she replied, nervously.

Zachary just looked at her then he shrugged. 'It's your money. Do as you like, I don't care. Just remember why they are called boom towns: one minute everyone is supposedly making a fortune, the next minute, all that's left is a huge mess.'

Their meal came and Clare was upset to see that Zachary's was already cut up for him. 'That it?' he asked between mouthfuls.

'No. By the time I write to my parents and convince them to lend me the money, it will be too late. So I was wondering if you could lend me some money,' she said in a rush.

'How much?'

'I have three thousand that I can get reasonably quickly, so. . . .'

'Seven thousand,' Zachary said, and Clare nodded.

'Why do you think I can get hold of seven thousand dollars quickly?'

'I don't know, I just thought. . . .'

'You realize that you need operating capital, too. Will Moose finish boring for you?'

'Yes, but he wants two dollars a foot to come back, that's twice what he usually charges.' A waitress came for their dishes. Zachary ordered coffee and pie for them both. He then just sat and looked at Clare. She found it unnerving. 'OK,' he said eventually.

Clare clapped her hands in excitement. 'Oh thank you, Zachary.'

'You'll need workmen.'

'Yes. There are two young men looking for work; they've worked on wells before. I can get them.'

'Watch that Moose. If he wants money just give him a bit. Don't get ahead of what he's done. I don't trust him.'

'Very well.'

Zachary stood and put money on the table. Clare grabbed his hand, 'Can't we go home, Zachary? Do you have to work?'

Zachary just looked at her. 'What do we do if we go home, Clare? Play the happily married couple?' He walked out.

It was around the oilfield in a flash, The Lady Clare now owned two oil sites. Not only that, she fully intended to work them herself. For a week, she and her men cleared the sites, built a shack, and waited for Moose to come with his drilling rig. It amazed Zachary, that she could work all day doing grubby jobs, yet she always looked clean and fresh.

At the end of the week. Zachary was at his desk, when a young man, he guessed about twenty-two, well dressed and wearing twin guns, came through the door. 'You Concannon?' he asked.

'Yes,' Zachary replied and continued writing. 'I'm James Lee, people call me Laredo.'

'Let me guess, you're from Texas.'

'Yes. You ever heard of me?' Zachary shook his head. 'Well I've heard of you. Didn't know that you had some parts missing, though.'

'That make a difference does it, Mr Lee?'

'It could. If I'm someone's deputy, I like to know that they can carry their share of the load.'

'You think I can't?'

'Don't know.'

Zachary stood and picked his revolver up from the desk and put it in his holster. 'When you're ready, Mr Lee.'

Laredo Lee smiled and went for his guns. He had them halfway out when he found himself looking down the barrel of Zachary's gun. 'Fair, Mr Lee, just fair. You're considered fast in Texas I suppose?' Zachary asked as he sat. 'Well, you Texas boys always were prone to beat your own drums. There's supposed to be two of you, where's the other one?'

Laredo Lee went to the door and said, 'Pete.' Another man, an older, more pallid version of

Laredo, stepped into the office. He wore a black suit and was carrying a Spencer .56-56 rifle. 'This here's Brother Pete,' Laredo said by way of introduction. 'He can shoot the eye out of a possum at two hundred yards.'

Zachary smiled. 'Well that's just grand if we get attacked by little furry animals. How is he at shooting men?'

Pete burst out laughing; when he finished, he just said, 'You point them out, I'll shoot them.'

Zachary observed him for a minute, 'Yes, I think you will,' he said eventually. Zachary swore both the brothers in. He asked what the town council had agreed to pay them. 'Five hundred a month each and a share of the fines. That's up to you, they said.' Zachary told the brothers that he got half and was happy to split his share equally with them. He showed them a list of what the fines were. 'This is where the money is, boys, so use your own discretion. Anyone gets lippy, fine them more; the town council doesn't mind, believe me.'

Laredo had moved to the door. 'Oh my God, I'm in love,' he said. 'Pete, look at this girl, and she's coming here. She must have heard that Laredo Lee's in town.'

He stood aside as Clare entered the office. 'Miss, I love you,' he said, after introducing himself. 'Would you marry me?'

Clare laughed. 'Heavens, Mr Lee, you do get right to it. Has it occurred to you that I might be married?'

'No, miss, I'm the only man good enough for you.'

'Well, I'm afraid I am married, Mr Lee, sorry.'

'You point him out and I'll shoot him.'

'I doubt that, Mr Lee; my husband is very good with a gun.'

'There's no one better with a gun than me, except him,' he said, nodding in Zachary's direction.

Clare smiled. 'Well, there you are, Mr Lee. Told you, you weren't good enough.'

'You're married to him?' Laredo asked in disbelief.

'Yes I am, Mr Lee.'

'What do you want, Clare?' Zachary asked abruptly.

'I need to buy some pipe for the wells. Moose is coming in a few days and he said to have pipe ready. Can I get some more money please? I'm sorry,' she added.

'Just go to the bank.'

'I don't like to go without asking first. I don't know how much you have.'

'It doesn't matter how much I have, Clare. Just smile at that young teller who always falls over himself trying to serve you; he'll give you every cent ever minted.' Zachary saw hurt in Clare's eyes, and felt no elation.

Clare was determined not to let strangers see that their relationship was under strain. 'Would you like to get something to eat?' she asked.

'I can't, I . . .' Zachary replied. He didn't get to finish because a grime-covered man rushed through the door.

'There's been an accident, Marshal,' the man said hurriedly. 'A heap o' pipes slipped and Moose is trapped by the legs. We tried to shift 'em, but when we do, they slip more.'

Zachary stood. 'OK, I'll be along.' To Clare, he said, 'Where's Sam?'

'Buck lost a shoe; Sam took him to the black-smith.'

Lester came in with the mail and Zachary introduced him to the Lee brothers. He asked Clare and Lester to wait outside. 'Just a few things,' he said to his new deputies. 'I do this job for the money, no noble motives, strictly for gain. So I don't expect my income to drop off just because you two are here. The only reason I wanted deputies, was so I didn't have to work twenty hours a day. When you fine someone, make sure you get the money: we don't give credit. If they don't have the money, take their horse, wagon, anything. Next, Lester lives here in the jail. He's a good man trying to get himself back on track. If you eat with him, I'd appreciate it if you wouldn't drink hard liquor in front of him. He's allowed one beer with his dinner. Don't let anyone pressure him into having a drink. Now you, Mr Laredo Lee, are flash. I don't like flash, I like quiet and businesslike, remember that. Finally, you seem very taken with Clare, so I'll tell you what the whole town knows: you touch her, I'll kill you. Is that clear?'

'Yes, Marshal, that's very clear,' Laredo replied.

'Good. Lester will take you to Ryan's and get you settled in. He likes to run things, so please be nice to him. I'll see you later.' Zachary left.

Laredo watched him go. 'What do you think?' he asked Pete, who shrugged. 'He's a bossy bastard.'

Pete laughed. 'Remember why we're here, Jimmy, money. Concannon gets offered all the big money jobs, and we're his deputies. Don't have to like him and not many people do. Those who don't, are shit scared of him. Either way, he gets it done. So we do the job, make a lot of money and buy our ranch, OK?'

'Sure, Pete, you know I'll do what has to be done. Sure is a pity about that Clare, though.'

Pete laughed again. 'Yeah, well remember what Concannon said about killing you; he's a man of his word, I'd guess.'

Outside, Zachary mounted his hired horse. 'Can I come with you?' Clare asked.

'You don't have a horse,' Zachary pointed out.

She held out her hand and stood expectantly. Zachary just watched her; then, to her delight, he bent down caught her under the arm and swung her up behind him. She sat sidesaddle with her arms around the husband she loved so much. This was good.

*

It was easy to find where the accident had occurred. A large group of men stood on a site that had been levelled for an oil well. Moose had been walking by when the pipes had rolled over the edge, taking him with them. Progress down the hill had been halted by a tree stump. It was a bad situation for Moose.

Zachary helped Clare down. 'Stay here,' he said.

She placed a hand on his arm, 'Be careful please?'

Zachary clambered down the slope which was strewn with lumber, pipes and tree stumps. He found Moose, as the man had said, pinned by the legs, under an unruly tangle of pipes. He was kneeling up and seemed to be holding the pipes back with just brute strength. 'Well, Mr Moose,' Zachary said. 'Quite a fix you're in, quite a fix.'

'You come to gloat?' Moose asked in a strained voice.

'Why would I want to gloat, Moose? Do you think I hold a grudge just because you beat the shit out of me while someone held me? Hardly. If I held a grudge, I'd have killed you. No, having you around is better than having a platoon of soldiers. Hell, I haven't had a fight since; just slapped a few loudmouths in the face with my axe handle. Who's going to take me on, knowing that I kicked the stuffing out of you? No one in his right mind, I'll tell you that. You getting tired?'

'Yes.'

'Well, if we try moving all this stuff, like as not,

you're going to get ironed out flatter than my Sunday shirt.'

'I know.'

Zachary turned to the watchers, 'I need someone with a shovel!' he yelled. No one moved to help.

'Won't one of you help, please?' Clare asked.

Clare looked around in desperation; still no one volunteered. Finally, a man in a suit and a floral waistcoat came forward, Max, Jenny's husband. He handed his coat to her and grabbed a shovel someone offered, 'Thank you,' Clare said, as he slipped and slid down the hillside.

'Shit,' Max said, when he saw Moose's predicament.

'What's the odds of him surviving?' Zachary asked.

'Three to one against,' Max replied.

'I'll have a hundred dollars on him.'

'Right, what's the plan?' Max asked. 'Dig him out?'

'No. Dig a hole big enough for him to lie in. Then he falls into it and the whole lot just rolls over him.'

'You're joking, right?' Moose asked.

'It's your life, Moose. If you have a better idea, I'm all ears.' He didn't.

Max set to digging. Zachary could see the strain was starting to tell on Moose, so, gently, he settled himself against the pipes. It took Max half an hour to dig the hole. On the hill, Clare and the ever growing crowd watched with bated breath.

'That looks about right,' Max said eventually.

'Yes,' Zachary replied. 'Right, Moose, soon as I move, the whole hill's going to be on top of you. So, be ready on three.' Zachary counted to three then jumped clear. On the hill, a collective groan went up. At last people were on the move, hurrying downhill as best they could, led by the crying Clare. Zachary had been struck a glancing blow and was bleeding from the head. 'How is he?' Zachary asked Max.

'He's OK; we just need to move a few lengths of pipe and he's good as new.'

Willing hands set to clearing the debris off Moose. Zachary was gathered into the arms of the crying Clare. 'Are you crazy?' she yelled at him. 'Look at you, you could have been killed. You only have one arm, Zachary, you can't do things like this.'

Zachary pushed away from her. 'Thank you, Clare. I needed reminding, thank you.'

'Oh, Zachary, I'm sorry. I was frantic. Look at you, you're all bloody and you look so tired. You're coming back to Ryan's, you're having a bath, then going to bed, no arguments. Your deputies can watch things.' Zachary nodded tiredly.

Men had moved the remnants of the pipes and helped Moose out of his shallow grave. He couldn't stand and had to be held up, but he insisted that his helpers take him to where Zachary still lay, being fussed over by Clare. 'Thanks, Marshal,' he said.

'Forget it. Just don't stuff Clare around.'

'I won't. I take a job I do it, just as long as I get paid.'

'You'll get paid; she has the money.'

'Right. I'd have started tomorrow, but I think it'll be a few days before I'm up and around again.'

Max came up and Moose thanked him, too. Max enquired if Zachary was all right. He didn't try to help Zachary up, Clare noticed.

'I owe you three hundred dollars,' Max said.

'For double or nothing, what number am I thinking of?'

Max studied him carefully. 'Eight,' he said eventually.

'Shit,' Zachary exclaimed. 'How come you can always do that?'

Max smiled and shrugged his shoulders.

'What if he'd said ten?' Moose asked.

'Then he'd have been thinking of ten,' Max replied.

Zachary got to his feet. Clare tried to help him. 'I can walk,' he said testily. 'I got hit in the head, not the feet.'

'I want to help you, Zachary,' Clare insisted, and put his arm around her shoulders and her arm around his waist.

'You can help by going back to Montana,' Zachary told her.

She matched his gaze. 'I won't go home without you.'

He pulled away from her and started up the

hill. 'Then you'll be missing from Montana for a long time,' he said.

Back in their rooms, Clare tried to hide the fact that she was upset by their argument by fussing, starting the water heater, then cleaning the wound on Zachary's head. She laid out clean clothes for him and insisted that for once he sleep on the bed, not the couch, as was his habit on the nights he came home. 'Don't worry, I won't molest you in your sleep,' she said. She thought she detected a glimmer of a smile. Zachary was sound asleep by the time Lester arrived, in a high state of agitation. He'd been giving the Lee brothers a tour of the town and had only just heard what had happened. It took several minutes of talking and a peep through the door, to assure him that Zachary was OK, just tired.

Lester sat in the parlour looking quite lost. 'I'm sorry, Clare,' he said. 'It's just that Zachary is my only friend. I look upon him as family. I lost my own in the first weeks of the war. My son David would have been Zachary's age now. I like to think that he would have been as fine a man as Zachary. My daughter would have been a bit older than you. She was a shy girl, not a fire-brand like you.'

Clare placed her hand on the old man's shoulder. 'I'm so sorry, Lester,' she whispered. 'You're wrong about only having one friend though.'

Lester patted her hand. 'Thank you. Look, I know it's probably none of my business, but I get the feeling that your relationship with Zachary isn't as good as it should be.'

'Is it that obvious?' Clare asked wistfully.

'It is, yes; is there anything I can do to help?'

'Just be his friend, Lester. Our trouble is something only we can work out, I'm sorry to say. Now, how about some lunch?'

Lester stood and smiled broadly. 'That I can do. I'll be the envy of every man in the town.'

Clare kept busy all afternoon. She arrived home about six, hoping Zachary might like to go out to dinner, but he was gone.

Two days later, a sick and sorry Moose came to the marshal's office. Zachary was sitting at his desk reading a letter. He looked up when Moose entered. 'What do you want?' Zachary asked.

Moose was momentarily lost for words. 'Well, I wanted to tell you that my men will move my rig on to your sites today. I'll be there tomorrow. My Ma and sisters are arriving today. I've rented a house. This is a nice town now and I'd like them with me. It'll be better than just sending Ma money.'

'The only thing stopping it from being a nice town before, was assholes like you, Moose.'

Moose smiled stiffly, 'Yeah. Well, it's amazing how a good kicking changes your outlook. Anyway, thanks for the other day. We'll start drilling tomorrow.'

'Tell Clare,' Zachary said, as he kept on reading. 'I'll be out of town for a few days, so don't stuff her around. If you want money just ask and she'll give you some. Not enough to get ahead of the work, though.'

'Fair enough.'

Moose still stood. Zachary looked up. 'What?'

'Oh, nothing. It's just that most people think that you and your wife don't get on all that well, yet you're mighty protective of her.'

Zachary stopped reading. 'And you would like me to discuss my personal life with you?'

'Well, if you want to talk to someone, I'll listen.'

Zachary laughed. 'I'll tell you this much, Moose. You remember the other day, I told you that I don't carry a grudge? Well, I lied, I do. You do anything to upset Clare, I'll take it very personally. That's all you need to know about us.'

'Fair enough. Just one last thing in return for saving my life: there's a man in town, Tom Toohey. I've struck him on other oil sites. He comes into town calling himself an investor, but all he ever seems to do is play poker. After a few weeks though, he suddenly owns a few oil wells. Always claims that the previous owner wanted to move on, go home, something. They always seem to conveniently disappear.'

Zachary listened carefully. 'You think he's a claim-jumper?'

'Nothing surer. Doesn't do it himself, but I've seen him in the company of some pretty rough-looking individuals. I reckon he picks on whoever he thinks is the weakest.'

'So, you think he'll pick on the only woman who owns wells, knowing full well she's my wife?'

'Yes, I do. He'll think he has you at a disadvantage. He'll get rid of you and get your wife's wells at the same time. Plenty of people in this town won't be sad to see you dead. Then the good times will be back.'

Zachary pondered this. 'What about my deputies?' he asked.

'One loudmouth kid and a rifleman? Couple of bushwhackers'll drop them in about two seconds.'

'Don't underestimate them; they come very highly recommended by people whose judgement I respect.'

'You'd know better than me. I'm just telling you what I think will happen.' When Moose left, Zachary sat and mulled over their conversation. He couldn't do anything about this Toohey person without proof. He looked up as Clare came through the door. She took his breath away, she was so beautiful. It seemed that her confidence had grown from working on her wells.

Clare was excited about something, but Zachary insisted that she come to where he kept all the confiscated weapons. He picked her out a Smith & Wesson short-barrelled .32. He made her promise faithfully to keep it with her at all times, no matter what, and to stay close to Sam. 'There's some men in town reputed to be claim-jumpers.

The gun is just a precaution. If anyone touches you, you shoot him,' Zachary told her.

Clare was still excited, her parents were coming to visit, they'd be here tomorrow, she told him.

'I'll probably miss them, I have to go out of town, tonight.'

Clare was upset at this. She knew that Zachary liked her parents, and they certainly liked him. She had hoped that if they could all spend some time together, it might help their relationship. 'You're not just saying that?' she enquired.

Zachary handed her a telegraph message he had received. It read: *In urgent need of lawman, beware of deputies*. It was signed Streeter.

'Streeter is the telegraph operator in a town called Boundary Bend, about two hundred miles away. Something's obviously wrong, so I'll go and take a look,' Zachary explained.

'Why you? Why now?' Clare asked. 'Because this is what I do,' Zachary replied rather sharply.

'I'm sorry, I just thought that it would be nice to spend some time with my parents.' Clare was exasperated and getting angry. 'Well, would you at least like me to tell them hello, say you're sorry you missed them, anything, for God's sake?'

'Yes, tell them to take you home and make you divorce me.'

'You bastard!' Clare yelled at him. 'I'll never do that, do you hear? Never.'

Zachary looked towards the door. Clare turned,

Lester stood there looking embarrassed. 'How did you get on?' Zachary asked.

Lester entered with Zachary's coat. 'I did the best I could.'

Zachary struggled into his coat. The right sleeve hung down like a dead weight. There was a glove protruding from it. 'What do you think?' he asked Clare. 'I'm going in disguise.'

'You look ridiculous,' Clare said, 'It just hangs there.' She thought for a moment. 'Get a bandage and make a sling, pretend you have a broken arm.'

'Good idea. To the shop, Lester, please.'

Lester scurried out, Zachary removed his coat. 'Look, I'm sorry about your parents. I'll be gone three or four days. Perhaps they'll still be here when I get back. Would you like to get something to eat?' he asked.

'Can you spare the time?' Clare asked facetiously.

Zachary's one eye became cold and hard, 'No, not really,' he replied and went back to his paperwork. Clare knew that she'd made a gaff. Rather than say anything she stormed out. This wasn't good.

Chapter Nine

As part of his disguise, Zachary took Lester with him. If a bad element had taken over the town, Zachary reasoned that no one would take Lester for a lawman, and a lawman wouldn't be travelling with someone who looked like a clerk. They were the only two who alighted in Boundary Bend. It was just on 8 a.m., and the town looked to be deserted. A hardcase, wearing a deputy's badge, stepped out of the station master's office and called, 'Hey, you.'

As Zachary and Lester walked towards him, another deputy came out on to the platform. Through the window, Zachary saw that the only other occupant of the office was the telegrapher. 'Yes?' Zachary asked when he reached the men.

'Who are you?' the deputy asked.

'I'm James Jones, this is my father Lester. I'm a salesman, I'm here on business.'

'What do you sell?'

'Axe handles, mostly,' Zachary replied.

The two deputies laughed. 'Axe handles? You make a living outa that?' one asked.

'Oh yes,' Zachary replied. 'Do you realize that there are about ten million homes in America, and every one has at least one axe. Then there are places of work. I also sell pick and hammer handles. Look, I'll show you one.'

The two deputies were highly amused. Zachary took his axe handle from the top of his carpetbag. 'Look at that, high class hickory,' he said, just an instant before he hit both men in the head, dropping them to the ground. He reached into his bag. 'I also sell manacles, jail cells, lots of things,' he continued, as he manacled the men's hands behind their backs.

The dumbfounded telegrapher informed them that he was Streeter. A gang of men had ridden into town and just taken over. They had badly beaten the marshal, had demanded money from all the town's businesses, and from people coming in and out of town. There were six men who called themselves deputies and their leader who had made himself marshal. His name was McKittrick.

'Bad McKittrick?' Zachary asked.

'Yes,' Streeter told him. 'You know him?'

'Heard of him; he's from Texas. Old bastard must have more lives than a cat. One of his men is Waco Grimes.' Zachary asked Streeter the disposition of the deputies. Two would be at the other end of town, two having breakfast in the saloon, and McKittrick would be in the marshal's

office. Zachary asked Streeter to stand guard over
the two deputies and complimented him for being
brave enough to send for help.

'Who are you?' Streeter asked.

'I'm Zachary Concannon, this is Lester Jones.'

'I thought. . . .'

'You're right,' Zachary said with a brief smile,
'This is my disguise.'

Zachary took his gun from his bag and hid it in
the sling on his arm. Then he and Lester headed
for the saloon. They found two deputies having
breakfast, watched by a bartender who had a
black eye.

'Who are you?' one deputy asked.

'I have a message from the other deputies,'
Zachary said.

'Spit it out then, mister.'

Zachary withdrew his gun. 'The message is, you
blink I'll kill you,' he told them.

Lester and the barman took the deputies' guns
and the barman hit one of the men none too
gently, across the face. 'Shackle them,' Zachary
said. They also gagged the two with their bandan-
nas, then marched them out of sight. Zachary told
the barman to watch them, but on no account to
shoot anyone until they had taken the last two.
He sent Lester to tell the remaining men that
they were wanted in the saloon. Zachary stood
against the wall just inside the door and waited.
Ten minutes later they arrived, roughly
propelling poor Lester in front of them. When

they were inside the saloon, Zachary stepped out and cocked his gun. 'Move and I'll kill you,' he said.

'You won't get us both,' one said.

'I think I will,' Zachary replied, as he clubbed him to the ground. The second man stood rooted to the spot. Lester and the barman shackled them both, as Zachary removed his coat.

'There's still McKittrick,' the barman said.

'I'll go get him. If he comes out of the jail instead of me, will you shoot him?'

'Yes, damned right I will. You're Concannon, aren't you?' the barman asked. 'You be careful, that McKittrick is bad news.'

The two men watched as Zachary crossed the street and walked down to the marshal's office. It seemed like minutes until two closely spaced shots rang out, then, a very short space of time until Zachary appeared on the sidewalk.

'Holy shit, he got him,' the barman said to a much relieved Lester.

They herded all the prisoners together. When they were told that McKittrick was dead, one almost went berserk. 'I'll kill you!' he screamed at Zachary. 'If it takes me years, I'll get you.'

'Let me guess, you're Waco Grimes, right?' Zachary said.

'Yeah. Bad was like a father to me, so you're dead, you bastard, it's only a matter of when!' Grimes screamed.

'Well, hell, Waco,' Zachary replied. 'I'd hate to

make you wait. I suppose you're the fastest gun to come out of Texas?' He laughed. 'I met Laredo Lee, recently, you faster than him?'

'Yeah, I'm the best.'

Zachary smiled a mirthless smile. 'Well, now we're getting somewhere.' He threw Lester the key, 'Unchain him please, Lester.' Lester shook his head and didn't move.

'Do it,' Zachary said sharply. Lester did so. Zachary picked up a revolver. 'Out in the street, Waco,' he said. To Lester, he said, 'If I go down, make sure you get the reward money for these bastards; should set you up for life.' To the bartender he said, 'You keep a bead on Waco, I go down, you drop him.'

'Yes, sir,' the barman replied.

The street was full of people brought out by the previous gunfire. Zachary stood twenty feet from Waco and threw the gun slowly through the air. He then drew his own revolver and held it on Waco until he had holstered the weapon. He then holstered his own gun. As soon as he had, Waco drew. He wasn't as fast as Laredo Lee and Zachary shot him through the chest before he had cleared leather. Zachary walked up to him and watched dispassionately as he died. 'Pity you Texas boys don't shoot as good as you talk,' he said.

The town celebrated as if it was a holiday. The town council immediately convened a meeting. The first item on the agenda was that they should claim any bounty money on the dead and captured outlaws. Zachary quickly put an end to that idea. 'You didn't get them, I did,' he told the mayor.

'But you're a lawman; this is your job,' someone protested.

'You listen and listen good,' Zachary told them. 'I do this for money, no other reason. I'm not interested in making your town a safer place to live, it's strictly for the cash. Another thing, get yourself a professional lawman, not some retired cowboy. I'll leave you a list of names.'

'How about you?' the mayor asked.

'Sure, I'll do it, if you can pay me more than I get at Pioneer Run, which is about two thousand a month.'

The council agreed that they couldn't pay that much.

Zachary and Lester stayed two days. They arranged for a judge to come and try the outlaws; arranged to have the reward money, which was $32,000, forwarded to Pioneer Run. Zachary promised Streeter $2,000, and the barman $1,000. Then he and Lester caught the train and went home.

They arrived back in Pioneer Run as quietly as they had left. People on the street gave them a wide berth and stared furtively, as they made their way to the office. The Lee brothers were sitting at the desk drinking coffee.

'Well, look who's here,' Laredo said. 'It's all over

town that you killed McKittrick and Grimes. Grimes was real fast, they say.'

Zachary dropped his bag, 'He wasn't as fast as you, Laredo, and we all know how fast that is don't we? There's a lesson here for you, young James, never underestimate anyone, never. It's not that I'm all that much faster than you, I'm not, but you just don't expect a man with one arm to be any good, at anything. I know men, who, if you cut both arms off, would bite you to death. Remember that. Everything quiet?'

'Yep,' Pete replied. 'Your wife has been in twenty times to see if you're back. Your in-laws were here, but they left for New York yesterday. They're very nice people.'

'Yes, they are. Well, Lester and I are going to get some breakfast, then I am going to have a sleep. By the way, the reward money on those bastards was thirty-two thousand. I paid out three thousand to two men in Boundary Bend and Lester insists that we share the rest with you two. Don't know why, you didn't do anything. So, you get fourteen thousand five hundred between you. Easiest money you ever made.'

When Zachary and Lester left, Laredo and Pete looked at each other and had a little laugh. 'This sure is going to be a good ranch,' Pete said.

After breakfast, Zachary returned to the hotel and bathed. He decided for only the second time, to sleep on the bed. Clare's subtle perfume filled his senses as he drifted off to sleep.

Clare headed for the jail, shortly after noon. To her great relief, she found Lester in one of the cells. He told her that Zachary had gone home. 'Is he OK?' she asked. Lester assured her that he was.

Clare found Zachary asleep on the bed. He looked totally relaxed, which was something she didn't often see. What Alice White had said, came back to her: 'He was a beautiful boy.' She sat gently on the bed and brushed his face softly with her hand. He was instantly awake and rolling off the bed, reaching for his gun, on a chair.

'It's OK, Zachary, it's me,' she said.

'You scared the shit out of me, Clare, I could have shot you!' he exclaimed forcefully.

'I'm sorry, I didn't mean to frighten you.' Zachary got up slowly. 'Don't go, please, let's talk. How was your trip?' Clare asked.

'You know how it was. It was in the paper; I killed two men.'

'I know, it must have been terrible for you.'

'Do you think so? Well, I'll tell you something. When I was about twelve, I had a grey pony, which fell when we were jumping a fence and broke his leg. My father made me destroy him. "A man must learn to do the hard things", he told me. That was the last time I was upset about killing anyone or anything. Killing anyone means no more than squashing a bug.'

'I don't believe that.' He didn't reply. There was a lull in the conversation. 'Would you like to do something? Perhaps you'd like to look at the wells,' Clare asked.

'Yes. We'll get something to eat, then you can take me out and show me these holes you're pouring money down at a great rate. That sound nice?'

'Don't be like that, please. And yes, that sounds very nice.'

On the way out, Clare told Zachary that she had been approached by a consortium, who wanted to build a pipeline to the rail depot. She would have to build a holding tank, and pay a proportion of the cost of the pipeline. She had tentatively engaged a man who was building the tanks. 'He builds them out of boards and caulks them like a ship. That means—'

'I know what caulking is, Clare, how much?'

'All up about eight hundred dollars,' she answered nervously. Zachary laughed.

After lunch in the saloon, they went out into the street. Buck was tied to the hitch rail; he neighed when he saw Zachary. 'He's getting fat, cut down on his feed a bit. Where's Sam?'

'He went to Jennie's with Lester. I told him I'd be perfectly safe with you.'

At the well site, Clare led Zachary around excitedly, showing him everything. Moose was piping the hole because it kept falling in. 'Wasn't unusual,' he said. Zachary was introduced to Clare's workers, Joe and Bob. Joe stared at him with a fair amount of enmity, Zachary thought.

Clare dragged him around both sites, then to

where the tank was to be built. They also discussed the cost of the pipeline with the other partners. Back at well one, as Clare called it, Moose informed them that in his opinion they would hit oil tomorrow. 'You can smell it in the soil,' he told them.

Clare was ecstatic. 'Isn't this exciting?' she asked happily. Zachary had to agree it was. Still Joe glowered at him.

Two days later, in the mid afternoon, Clare rushed into the marshal's office. This was the first time Zachary had seen her when she didn't look as fresh as a spring morning. Her blouse was grubby and her hair unruly. 'We struck oil, Zachary!' she informed him. 'You should have seen it, it just shot out of the ground. Twenty barrels a day, Moose thinks, you should have seen it,' she repeated.

'I'm glad for you, Clare,' Zachary told her, and he was.

'I'm taking everyone concerned to dinner at Jennie's, she'll cook something special. Will you come too, please?'

'I can't, I'm sorry. I have to go to the eastern slope. There's been a fire, people are dead.'

Clare looked crestfallen, 'You're not just saying that?'

'Look out the damn door, Clare, see the smoke? You can't possibly miss it.'

'I'm sorry. Yes, I've seen the smoke. What time

will you be back, do you think?'

'I don't know. If I'm not too late I'll join you for dinner. I'll take Buck. If you go out to the well again, you'll have to hire a horse.'

It was near to midnight when Zachary got home. He bought a bottle of whiskey from the bar and retired to their rooms. By the time he had lit the water heater and had a few drinks, he heard the door open. He heard Clare say, 'Goodnight, Joe.'

'Clare, I love you. Let's go away together,' Joe said.

Clare was momentarily speechless apparently. Then she answered, 'Joe, I'm a married woman.'

'He doesn't love you!' Joe replied vehemently. 'Everyone knows that. He makes you work. Why do you put up with him?'

'Everyone is wrong then, Joe. Zachary doesn't make me work, he allows me to do what I like. Where do you think I got the money to do what I've done? Whose money pays you, Joe? It's Zachary's. That's the trouble with most of you men. You think that a woman should be content to keep house and raise children. What if she's not?'

Before any more could be said, Zachary opened the door. 'Oh, hello, dear,' he said to Clare. 'Brought a friend home have you? Would you like me to go downstairs, while you entertain him?'

He saw hurt in her eyes. 'Don't, Zachary, please,' she whispered.

'You don't deserve her!' Joe yelled at him.

'I agree,' Zachary replied.

'I'd look after her.'

'How, Joe? Sell her wells and live on her money?'

'Damn the wells, we'd manage.'

Zachary laughed. 'You'd manage, that sounds grand. Living in a shack somewhere while you scrounge for a few dollars. Clare would love that. But, of course, I forgot, you've met Clare's parents and you know they own half of Montana. See Clare as your ticket to a fortune do you, Joe? Well, off you go, I hope you'll be very happy.' Zachary shut the door and went back into the room. Clare followed shortly. 'You going?' Zachary asked from where he stood at the table, pouring himself a drink.

Clare flew at him. 'You bastard!' she screamed, and tried to slap him. He swayed out of the way and caught her by the arm. She couldn't tell what he was thinking, but for the first time since she had met him, she was scared of him. She fought back tears. Then he just let her go and took a drink.

'You getting drunk?' Clare asked, as she massaged her wrist.

'No, my love, I don't get drunk. I was drunk for six months after Cold Harbour, now it has no effect. Pity.' Zachary went to bathe and change, his clothes reeked of smoke. Clare sat on the sofa, desperate to find a way to repair their relationship, which seemed to be at an all-time low.

At a knock on the door, Clare opened it, to find the mayor and a minister, standing there. They wanted to see Zachary, so she invited them in. Both men accepted a whiskey when she offered it. It surprised her that the preacher would so readily accept a drink. When Zachary came into the parlour, the mayor introduced the minister as the Reverend Day. 'Call me Robert,' he said.

'What do you want, Reverend?' Zachary asked rather pointedly. 'Are you going to give me a lecture on the fifth commandment?'

'No, Zachary, we just thought that you might like to talk, or might just like some company.'

'What happened?' Clare asked with great concern.

'I executed a man,' Zachary replied.

'Oh, my God, what happened?' Clare asked.

'He was terribly badly burnt. His face and hands were burnt down to the bone. He asked me to put him out of his misery, so I wrapped him in a blanket and shot him through the head.'

Clare sat with her hands to her face as tears coursed down her cheeks. The mayor and the minister were visibly shocked at Zachary's graphic description.

'I don't know what to say to you,' the minister said.

'Don't say anything, Reverend. Go pray for the soul of the deceased, I don't need any help from you.'

After an awkward silence, the visitors left.

Zachary sat on the sofa with his eyes closed, his drink in his hand.

Clare knelt by him. 'Zachary, please let me help you,' she whispered.

'I don't need help, Clare, can't you get that through your head? Why don't you go off with your boyfriend? Or go back to Montana and marry one of those farm boys. Just leave me alone, that's all I ask, just leave me alone.'

Clare barely saw Zachary now, as he lived almost exclusively at the jail. She had come to the conclusion that their relationship was irreparable. The second well produced oil a week later, but Clare didn't even bother to tell him.

Three days after this, Bob, Clare's other workman, rushed into the jail, where Zachary talking to the Lee Brothers. He was in a high state of excitement. 'Marshal, Marshal,' he blurted out, 'men came to the wells and are holding Clare as a hostage. They want you. They said that if you don't come immediately, they'll kill her.'

The Lee boys sprang into action, Pete grabbed for his rifle and was halfway to the door when Zachary called, 'No! I'll go; they want me. You two get uphill of the wells. If I go down, you drop anyone who's left standing. For God's sake, don't shoot Clare or Sam.'

The brothers looked at each other. They knew only too well what the general opinion was of Zachary's relationship with Clare, yet here he was showing concern for her wellbeing. He had stuck another revolver in his belt. 'You going or not?' He asked them as he headed for the door.

'It's done,' Pete said.

Zachary gave them a smile. 'Thanks,' he said as he left.

Zachary rode Buck at breakneck speed across country to the well site. People working on their wells were astounded to see the big bay horse at flat gallop across the side of the hill, jumping anything in its way. They all marvelled at the control a one-armed man had on his flying steed.

At well one, Zachary found Clare being held by a man who had a gun to her head. There was also another man with a rifle. 'I'm here, now let her go,' he said as he dismounted.

'Not likely, Marshal,' the man replied. 'She's mine now. She's gonna sign her wells over to us and I'm gonna keep her. Part of the spoils.'

'Come on, let her go, she can't even cook.'

The man grinned evilly. 'I don't want her for her cookin', I'll teach her what I want her to know. She ain't learnin' it from you, accordin' to what people say. Then, when I'm sick of her, I'll rent her out. Woman with her looks should have fifteen years or so before she starts lookin' old. After that, I'll take her south, sell her to an Injun.'

'That's assuming that you live that long.'

'Oh, I'll live that long. See, I think you're all mouth. People just feel sorry for you with your one arm and one eye. I reckon I could take you any time. But the people I represent, they've insisted on bringin' in a gunfighter, says he knows you.'

'Who are you representing? Tom Toohey?' Zachary asked. By the look on the man's face, Zachary knew that he was right.

Before the man could answer, another man stepped out of the shack. 'Hello, Zachary,' he said.

'Well, well, Luke Armstrong. I thought you were in Kansas.'

'Was, Zachary, but hitting cowboys over the head for a hundred dollars a month isn't the job for a man with my talents.'

'So you're hiring out? Why not take on a boom town, good money to be made.'

'Good money hiring out, Zachary. I'm getting paid five thousand to drop you. See, I want to be a Southern gentleman like you could be. A few more jobs like this and I'll have enough.'

Zachary smiled. 'I doubt it, Luke; it takes more than money. You got the five thousand on you?'

'Yes, why?'

'Because you're fined five thousand dollars for disturbing the peace. Pay up and leave, or die. Your choice.'

Luke Armstrong smiled then went for his gun. All the watchers on the hill were astounded when Zachary Concannon, the marshal they either loved or hated, easily outdrew the gunfighter, who collapsed to the ground, a red stain spreading slowly over his crisp white shirt.

The man holding Clare started to retreat,

Zachary swung on him, 'Down!' he yelled at Clare, who wrenched herself out of the man's grasp and fell to the ground. Zachary shot the man dead. Another gunman broke from the shack, and he and the other man who had been with Clare began to run blindly. From up the slope, two shots rang out and the men went down and lay still.

Clare was up, running and crying. Zachary caught her and held her. 'It's all right, I've got you,' he said into her hair.

Clare's worker, Joe, rushed from the shack, but pulled up short when he saw Zachary holding Clare. He was followed by Sam, who was holding a bloody bandanna to his head.

'You're supposed to be watching her!' Zachary yelled at Sam.

'They got me in the shack, hit me over the head. I had no chance.'

'Sorry, are you hurt?'

'I'll live.'

Men on the slopes converged on Clare and Zachary, still in an embrace. Zachary asked some of them to get the gunfighter's body on to a horse. 'You OK now?' he asked Clare, softly.

'Yes,' she replied into his chest. 'Just hold me, please.'

'I've got you,' he told her. To the watchers he said, 'These men are dead, not because they tried to kill me, but because they assaulted my wife. I told you when she first arrived what would happen if anyone touched her, now you know that I was serious.'

The Lee brothers joined the milling throng and Zachary thanked them and told them to get whatever money the men had. Nearly $8,000 all up.

'They wanted you dead real bad,' Pete commented. To Pete Lee, Zachary said, 'Can you take Clare and Sam back to Ryan's please? Anyone looks sideways at Clare, you shoot him. Better get the doc to have a look at Sam's head.'

'Done,' the taciturn Pete replied.

Zachary disengaged himself from Clare. 'You go with Pete,' he said gently.

'Please don't leave me,' Clare pleaded.

'You'll be safe with Pete. I have business to take care of.'

'Please come home tonight then, please?'

'OK, when I can. You come with me,' he said to Laredo.

Zachary and Laredo mounted up, Laredo riding double with the body of Luke Armstrong. They rode to Turner's, a large gambling tent, where Zachary knew that he would find Tom Toohey. He slung the body over his shoulder and walked into the tent. The din inside ceased immediately. It was easy for Zachary to find Tom Toohey, who was by far the best-dressed man in the place. Zachary walked up to where Toohey sat and dropped the body on the table, spilling cards and poker chips everywhere.

'Shit!' Tom Toohey exclaimed, as he sprang

from his chair. As he did, Zachary drew his gun and clubbed him to the ground. He drew back the hammer. 'I don't care that you hired a gunman to kill me, but you sent men to manhandle and terrorize my wife. For that, you die.'

As Tom Toohey cringed on the ground, Laredo put his hand on Zachary's arm. 'You can't just shoot him, Zachary,' he said, gently. It was the first time he had ever called him Zachary. 'We're lawmen, not murderers.'

'Get his money,' Zachary said eventually.

Laredo laughed, 'That's more like it,' he said, and searched Tom Toohey's pockets. 'Another five thousand; a good day.'

Zachary turned his attention to Tom Toohey. 'You get out of town. If I ever see you again, I'll kill you.'

Back in their rooms, Clare cleaned and bandaged the wound on Sam's head. An idea had come to her and she hurried to find Margaret Ryan. She told Margaret that she wanted to cook dinner for herself and Zachary. Margaret was most helpful and gave her a chicken and vegetables and unrestricted use of the kitchen. Clare laid the table in their parlour, had a bottle of champagne on ice, everything for a romantic dinner for two, only Zachary didn't come home. At about eleven, Margaret informed her that the chicken was turning to cinders. Clare told her to give it to anyone who came in late.

Zachary arrived home a bit after midnight. Clare was asleep on the sofa. The table was laid and there was a bottle of wine in a bucket of water. He shook Clare awake. 'Been entertaining, have you?' he asked.

'Don't start, please,' Clare asked in desperation. 'No, I haven't been entertaining. I had hoped to show you that I can cook, but you didn't come home. You said you would.'

'I did, Clare, I'm here now. I'm sorry about dinner; if you'd told me, I'd have tried to be early.'

'Wouldn't have been a surprise then, would it?' Clare replied. She stood. 'Thank you for today.'

'Think nothing of it,' Zachary replied.

For two weeks, Zachary and Clare maintained an uneasy truce. He came home most nights, but she didn't offer to cook anything, and he didn't ask her to.

One Wednesday night he was home shortly before ten. Clare was obviously very nervous about something, and was pacing up and down.

'What's wrong with you?' Zachary asked.

'I've had an offer for the wells and our share in the pipeline,' she told him nervously.

'And?' Zachary asked.

'I don't know, it's nearly all your money that I've spent, we should decide together.'

'How much?'

'Two hundred and twenty-five thousand dollars,' Clare told him breathlessly.

'Good heavens above,' Zachary replied. 'So what's the problem? That's a huge profit in no time at all, really. You've spent what? Twenty thousand?'

'About. I didn't know that you kept count,' Clare replied with a strained smile.

'Well, I did. So, I ask you again, what's the problem?'

'There's no problem. Talk is though, that oil could reach twelve dollars a barrel in the next few months. With both wells producing about twenty barrels a day, there's a fortune to be made.'

'Talk can be wrong though, Clare. Don't forget oil has been as low as one dollar. If I were you, I'd take the money. You can't possibly make this percentage of profit again. You can go home and buy the other half of Montana.'

'Will you come with me?' He shook his head. 'Then I'm staying.'

'Suit yourself. But I think it's only fair to tell you that I'm pulling out. I'll wait until you sell out, if that's what you decide to do, but after that, I'm gone.'

Clare was dumbfounded, 'Where are you going?' she asked once she had regained her composure. 'Home to Richmond?'

'No, I've taken the job as marshal of Wichita, Kansas.'

'Good God, why?' was all she could think of to ask.

'Because it's what I do, Clare. There's no one

here to worry about anymore. The Lees can keep the peace here, with their eyes closed. Wichita will pay me as well as I'm paid now, and, who knows, I might actually find one of those big-mouthed Texas boys who's as good with a gun as he thinks he is.'

Clare just sat and stared; she couldn't believe what she was hearing. Looking for someone good with a gun? Then it suddenly hit her. 'Oh, my God,' she said in disbelief, 'you're trying to find someone fast enough to kill you.'

'Don't be ridiculous,' Zachary replied defensively.

'It's true. Why else would you be looking for someone who's fast with a gun?

For some time Zachary just stared at her. 'So what?' he yelled finally. 'So what if I am? Do you have any idea, how much I hate being like I am? How I hate taking half an hour to get dressed? How I hate having to get my meals cut up for me? But do you know what I hate the most? I hate you. I hate knowing that people look at you and wonder why the hell would a woman like you, marry a one-eyed cripple.'

Clare rose from where she sat and stood in front of her husband, who had finally dropped his defences and admitted how he truly felt. 'Zachary,' she said softly. 'You know why I married you, for the most selfish of reasons, to get myself out of trouble. I want to stay married to you because I love you. It doesn't matter what people think; you told me that when you rescued me from Lou. It doesn't matter that I'll have to cut your meals up, either. All that matters is that I love you and you love me. I know you do; you told my father.'

'I didn't tell your father that, Clare, he just assumed it.'

'Then look me in the eyes and tell me that you don't. If you convince me, I'll go home as soon as I've sold the wells and divorce you immediately.'

'I don't love you, Clare,' Zachary said rather lamely. 'Go home and divorce me. I want you to live up to our agreement.'

Clare laughed gaily and reached up and kissed him on the cheek. 'That was pathetic, Zachary, absolutely pathetic. Now I know you do love me. If you go to Wichita, I'll follow you.'

'I'll go somewhere else, then.'

'You go where you like, my love. Go to hell. But when you turn around, your loving wife will be right there behind you, so get used to it. Now, I haven't had dinner yet and you are going to take me. And tell Jenny, your wife will cut yours up.'

Chapter Ten

For the next ten days or so, Clare was engrossed in the sale of the wells. During this time, she and Zachary seemed to have reached an impasse. He never spoke of Wichita and neither did she. He was most supportive with regard to the sale, although he insisted she do the business, 'They're your wells,' he said.

At times, their relationship was almost pleasant. They were invited to a Thanksgiving dinner and dance by the mayor. It was a pleasant evening and Zachary obviously enjoyed himself. But then there were times when he was very distant, and some nights when he didn't come home.

Clare had the feeling that the men to whom she was selling her wells were trying to take advantage of the fact that she was a woman. This was borne out when, on arriving at well one, one morning, she found strange men had taken over. They leered at her and made suggestive remarks. She rode to the jail and told Zachary what had happened. He took her firmly by the arm and marched her to the office of the prospective buyers.

There were four men having a meeting when Zachary and Clare burst into the room. Zachary told them in no uncertain terms to get their men off the well site, or he'd do it for them.

'We have contracts, we have rights,' one man said.

'You don't have shit until Clare signs the contracts, and she won't do that until she sees the money,' Zachary told him.

'There's been a minor hold up,' one man told them.

'Has there?' Zachary replied. 'Well, let me tell you something: I know what you're up to, you want to control the pipeline, that's where the money is, but you can't do that until you have Clare's section. Without that, you have nothing.'

'That's not illegal, Concannon,' someone said.

'No, but what is illegal, is you trying to take over before you've paid Clare. Now, you have until this afternoon to come up with the money. Next, you send someone out to the wells and tell your men to disappear. You tell them, that not so long ago, men insulted Clare, and I killed two of them and my deputies killed another two. If they haven't gone by the time we get out there, I'll kick the shit out of them. Is that clear?'

'You're bluffing,' someone said.

Zachary smiled and leaned on the table. 'Mister,

I've only known you for a few minutes and I don't like you. So I'll tell you something about myself. I've been in a real bad mood for about the last ten years. If I have to come back, your futures don't look bright.' He stood up. 'Clare will be back at three o'clock. Have her money, cash or bankdraft.'

Back at well one, the strange men were leaving when Zachary and Clare arrived. They looked as though they might stand and fight until Zachary backed Buck into them, then they ran. Zachary chased them, as they made their way through the oilfield. When he caught them, he rode them down, much to the delight of onlookers. At three o'clock, Clare got her money.

The next day, Clare paid off her men. She gave them each a bonus of five thousand dollars.

'Well, I guess this is goodbye,' Joe said, when they were alone. 'I don't suppose there's any point me going to Montana,' he queried.

'Absolutely none, Joe. Look, don't make things hard for yourself. You have good money now. Go back to Tennessee and buy yourself that farm you want, you'll find a nice girl.'

'She won't be you, though. God, I wish I'd gone to Montana before him.'

Clare reached out and touched Joe on the cheek. 'Joe, you're a lovely man, but there is something you must understand. Zachary is the man I was born to marry, I truly believe that. I was probably proposed to half a dozen times before Zachary came along, but I waited for him.

It doesn't matter if people don't think we get on, he is my husband, until death us do part. Things got off to a very rocky start for us, for reasons I'm not prepared to discuss with anyone, but I love him very much. If anything should happen to him, I very much doubt that I will ever marry again. So it could never have been you, Joe, I'm sorry.'

Close to tears, Joe just looked at her. 'Goodbye, good luck,' he said and turned away.

'You too, Joe,' Clare said to his back.

Clare was worried that Zachary would do as promised and leave for Wichita. A few days later, she and Sam were on the boardwalk outside Ryan's, passing the time with Lester and the Lee brothers, when Zachary rode up.

'Have to go to Stewart's, been a riot apparently,' he told them. 'What are you two up to?' he asked the brothers.

'We're going to have some breakfast,' Laredo told him.

'Weren't you called out to the eastern slope?'

'Yeah, we went early; nothing. A wild-goose chase.'

Zachary reined away. 'OK, see you later.'

'You will be back, Zachary?' Clare called after him.

'Perhaps,' he said.

They all stood and watched the enigmatic man, as he rode on down Main Street. All of them were lost in their private thoughts about him. They noticed that he tipped his hat to any women he passed, and spoke to several men. The townspeople loved him, the oilfield people tolerated him. Everyone acknowledged that he did the job without fear or favour.

Zachary was well past the livery stable, when a volley of shots rang out and he was thrown from the saddle. 'Oh shit!' Pete Lee exclaimed, as they started to run.

Only Clare stood, until she saw Zachary scramble to cover behind a pile of lumber. Then she, too, was running.

'Rifles, get rifles!' Sam yelled.

At the jail, Laredo was already out with rifles for himself, Sam and Clare. 'Where the hell are they?' he asked.

As if in answer, a man broke from cover and ran to try and outflank Zachary. Before any of them could move, a shot rang out from where Zachary was sheltering. The man fell and lay still.

'Thank God,' Clare whispered to herself.

'We'll take the high ground, you stay here,' Laredo said, and he and Pete ran off.

Nothing moved. From up the slope two shots rang out. A man was running down the hill. Clare and Sam raised their rifles and fired together. The man stumbled and fell, then lay still. More firing rang out from up the hill. Now the Lee brothers were in sight, making their way down the slope, one always covering the other. Then they were out

on the road. It seemed as if all the attackers were
dead.

Clare started forward, but Sam grabbed her,
'Not yet,' he said.

There was a slight movement from where
Zachary was hiding behind the heap of lumber.
First, a hand holding a gun appeared, then, slowly,
Zachary stood. He started to move very lethargi-
cally. His shirt, which had been white, was now
crimson, except for half the left sleeve. His blue
denim trousers were black down to his gunbelt. He
took a few faltering steps then collapsed, dropping
his gun. With a last great effort he screamed,
'Clare!' at the top of his voice, before pitching
forward and lying still.

Now there was movement. The woman that
they all knew as The Lady Clare was running,
holding up her skirt, leaping objects like a young
deer fleeing through the forest. Clare cradled
Zachary in her arms, his blood soaking her skirt
and blouse.

Zachary tried to speak. 'I—' he said, trying to
stave off oblivion until he had finished.

'I know,' she said against his cheek, soaked by
her tears, 'Why did you have to get shot to pieces
before you could tell me?'

Zachary smiled slightly, and with one last
tremendous effort, he reached up and touched her
on the face, then he passed out, his breath coming
in shallow gasps.

*

Zachary knew he was hit and hit badly, and it hurt like hell. Funny, he'd been wounded before, and it had hurt, too. But losing his eye, nothing, just a blur. Didn't have a clue, until the doctor said, 'Your eye's gone, son,' then moved on.

Even when he lost his arm, he had heard the explosion, had seen the man behind him go down, but had felt nothing. All he knew was that he had dropped his saddle-bags. He couldn't lose them, they held his few personal belongings and his treasured gifts for Ben and Jos. He looked down and there they were, still clutched firmly in his hand, only his hand was on the ground with half his arm. The pain came later. The greatest pain was knowing that for the rest of his life, he would have to manage with one arm. Never again could he hold a woman in his arms. If he ever found someone compassionate enough to marry him, he would never be able to hold a baby and cluck it under the chin, the way all normal people did. For the rest of his life, people would look at him as though he was a freak.

Drink didn't help either. For six months, he had been blind drunk, but he couldn't kill himself with drink, and he wasn't strong enough to shoot himself. The only thing in his life that gave him any joy at all was Buck.

He'd been four years old when Zachary had first seen him. An outlaw that no one could handle, in a pen so small he couldn't turn around or lie down. He just had to stand there, completely helpless. Zachary had felt an empathy with him, so strong that he had bought him. Perhaps the horse felt it too. Perhaps the horse knew that here was a man who knew what it was like to be in a situation not of his own making, and who had no insight into his future. Buck had been a wonderful horse to train. He'd broken in like a dream and, from the outset, he was used to a man with one arm. It was as though he knew that the commands he would be given by Zachary, would be different from any others he'd ever receive. In fact, he didn't like being ridden by anyone else, except Clare. Clare. Perhaps old Buck could sense that his master loved her. Perhaps he could feel the goodness and life in this woman on his back. Perhaps he knew, when they rescued Clare, that riding him around, using her legs and heels to guide him, was the greatest thing an animal could do for a human.

Out of the corner of his eye, Zachary saw a man running to outflank him, he rolled on to his right side and shot him dead.

Thoughts of Clare came back to him. Thoughts of how easy it was to hurt her. Thoughts of how determined she was to make him understand that they could have a life together. And she was succeeding. But how could he suddenly tell her that he did love and want her? That he had loved her from the moment he had seen her standing on the porch at Top Hat. It made him smile to know that she had told Sam to hang around in the hallway, just in case he was needed. Now that wasn't ladylike, practical, but not ladylike. From up the hill he heard rifle shots. That would be the Lees. Good boys, the Lees. Laredo young and brash; Pete older and much more experienced. Rode with the Texas Brigade if Zachary was any guess. Seen his share, too. Liked to get the job done with as little fanfare as possible.

More shooting; two closely spaced shots, couldn't tell what that was. Feeling bad now, hit three times at least. Shit. How unlucky can one man be? How will his family feel if he dies. Will the anger finally subside and will they grieve for a lost son and brother? He tried to laugh: only until they find that I've left the estate to Artemus, and he has promised solemnly not to bow to pressure, not to return control to Father.

Artemus, poor sickly Artemus. The little brother he had had to carry around as a child. He was too weak to walk far. But he had been a marvellous companion. When he'd announced that he would fight for the Union, Artemus was the only one who understood why. When he'd left home, it was Artemus who had bid him farewell, who had held him in his arms and said, 'No matter what, we're brothers.' It was Artemus, who, through tireless enquiries, had located Ben and Jos.

He felt he was failing rapidly now. He was soaked in blood. How much could you lose before you died? he wondered. No more shooting. It didn't hurt anymore, perhaps that was a good sign, perhaps he would finally find peace. No more frightful head pains from his eye; no more pain from where his arm should be. Only one more thing he wanted to do in his life. He had to stand. He pulled himself up and forced himself to walk. A few steps and down he went, strength almost gone. Just enough for one last effort, 'Clare!' he screamed and toppled forward.

He knew Clare was holding him, holding him and crying. He was trying so desperately to tell her he loved her, but the words wouldn't come, but she knew.

'I know, I know, I love you, too. Why did you have to get shot to pieces before you could tell me?'

He couldn't answer, all he could do was touch her cheek, before darkness descended.

'Would someone help me, please!' Clare screamed at the crowd, as she held the lifeless form of her husband.

The Lee brothers and Lester, pushed their way through the mass of people. Lester collapsed to his knees crying uncontrollably. 'We need a litter,' Sam said.

There was movement in the crowd and the huge figure of Moose pushed through. 'I'll take him,' he said, then bent and scooped Zachary up, as if he was a baby.

Clare helped the distraught Lester to his feet, 'Lester, go get the doctor and Jenny, and ask them to come to our rooms, please. Can you do that?'

'Yes,' he said, and stumbled away.

The entire crowd started to move towards the saloon, the Lee brothers clearing a path for Moose. Further up Main Street, a horseman broke from the alley between the mercantile and the bank, then raced away. 'It's Toohey!' someone yelled.

Pete Lee stepped to the middle of the road. 'Get out of the way!' he commanded, as he brought his rifle to his shoulder. When he had a clear target, he fired. A .56-56 Spencer rifle fires a 350 grain bullet at a muzzle velocity of 1,200 feet per second. It was about a second and a half from when Pete pulled the trigger to when the bullet slammed into Tom Toohey's back, right between his shoulder blades. It killed him instantly. He stayed upright in the saddle for about five more seconds, then he fell to the dusty roadway and lay still. Laredo had been right, Pete could shoot the eye out of a possum at 200 yards.

Moose carried Zachary up the stairs and laid him on a table that had been hastily brought in and covered with a sheet. Moose's chest heaved from the effort of carrying Zachary so far. Clare thanked him and asked would he please clear everyone out of their rooms, except for the Lees, Sam and Lester when he returned. The big man had tears in his eyes and Clare didn't know if they were from emotion or exhaustion.

'He'll be OK,' Moose said. 'The bastard's too mean to die.' All Clare could do in reply was to hug him and pat his back.

Lester arrived with Jenny and Max. 'Oh, God,' Jenny said, then took control of the situation. She had Lester light the water heater and her husband tear up sheets for bandages, as she and Clare undressed Zachary.

By the time they had Zachary's clothes off, the doctor had arrived. Zachary had been hit four times: once through the right shoulder, and once through the stump of his arm. Another had hit him on the left shoulder, close to his neck and above the collarbone. The fourth, and by far the worst wound, was on his left side just below his ribs, and there was no exit wound.

'He's lost so much blood,' the doctor told them, 'but I have to go after this bullet. I must tell you, Clare, that his chances aren't good. He has virtually no chance if I leave the bullet in. Infection will set in and he'll be dead in a few days. If I operate, the shock might kill him. It will take a huge effort on his part to survive. So, tell me, what do I do?'

'You operate, Doctor,' Clare replied without hesitation. 'And he will live. I'll have no more talk of him dying, do you hear? No more!' she screamed. Sam came forward and held her.

The doctor and Jenny set to, washing Zachary down. They dressed the lesser wounds, both entry and exit, then started the operation. 'Get some whiskey,' the doctor said.

For half an hour the doctor probed for the bullet to no avail. Jenny stood alongside him soaking up blood and occasionally wiping his brow. 'Damn!' the doctor exclaimed, and threw his probe into a dish of whiskey. 'I'll have to open him up a bit,' he told them, as he reached for his scalpel. At times, it seemed as though the doctor had his whole hand inside Zachary, as he pushed and probed. After what seemed an eternity, he stopped. 'Got you,' he said joyously. 'Got you, you son of a bitch.'

Jenny held the probe while he followed it along with a pair of forceps. After nearly an hour, he dropped the offending bullet into a dish. He swabbed the wound, then sewed it shut. Then he took a swig of whiskey. 'Now we pray,' he told everyone.

Chapter Eleven

For a week Zachary lingered in and out of consciousness. Clare and Lester took turns in watching over him. The doctor visited daily, happy with Zachary's progress. There was no infection and Zachary's pulse and heartbeat were good.

Nine days after Zachary was shot, Clare and Lester were having breakfast together, in the kitchen. The saloon was busy with people eating, and wellwishers. There seemed to be a lull in the level of noise, Michael Ryan hurried to the kitchen. 'Come quick,' he said to Clare.

She and Lester hurried into the bar. Everyone was silent and staring. Clare looked up. Halfway down the staircase, Zachary stood, holding a blanket around himself. 'I'd like something to eat and someone to light the hot water heater for me, please,' he croaked.

Clare burst into tears and ran to him, holding him and crying uncontrollably. 'You shouldn't be up,' she said, once she'd regained some of her composure.

'It seems as if I've been awake forever. I didn't know where you were. Do you know where my eyepatch is?'

Clare laughed and cried, 'You lost it somewhere; we'll get you a new one. The doctor says you shouldn't wear it all the time. He thinks your eye wouldn't weep as badly if you let the air get at it. It doesn't matter to me how it looks. Now, come back upstairs: I'll get you some breakfast and fix you a bath.'

The doctor was astounded that Zachary was strong enough to get out of bed. 'He must have great inner strength,' he liked to say. He allowed Zachary to sit on the balcony in the sun and receive visitors, of which there were many.

The ladies brought food. So much, that they established a free food bar. It was amazing how popular beer and cake became. On the fourth day, Zachary was asleep for most of the afternoon. Clare spent her time writing letters to Artemus and her parents, informing them of Zachary's progress. At about 8 p.m., Clare brought Zachary something to eat. He dozed off again and Clare went to bathe and change. When she came out of the bathroom, he was awake again.

'How do you feel?' she asked.

'Good, thank you. Quite good, in fact.'

Clare turned down the lamp and sat on the edge of the bed. 'Zachary,' she said nervously, 'there's something we need to get settled between us.'

'I've told you a hundred times, Clare, I don't want any of the money. You did all the work on the wells, the money's yours.'

Clare laughed huskily and bent forward and kissed him gently. 'Believe me, Zachary, this has nothing to do with money.'

When Clare awoke, Zachary was lying on his side watching her.

'Hello,' she said snuggling close. 'How do you feel?'

'Exhausted,' he replied.

She laughed and hit him. 'Well at least now you can't divorce me,' she told him.

'I don't know about that. How about taking advantage of an invalid?'

'You weren't too much of an invalid last night.'

'No, oh well. Look, Clare, I want to say—'

Clare put a finger to his lips. 'Don't, Zachary; no apologies, we both made mistakes. But now everything is perfect.'

'It's not perfect, Clare, and it never will be. I'm still a one-armed man; do you know how much that limits what I can do?'

Clare propped herself up on one elbow and said, 'We'll manage, Zachary, we'll manage.'

They lay in silence for a while, until eventually, Zachary said, 'I've been thinking, if we leave in the next few days, we could be back in Montana for Christmas.'

'What about Wichita?' Clare asked.

'They'll get someone else. Besides, one of those Texas boys might be real good with a gun.'

Clare laughed and cried, all at once. 'We can go to Richmond if you'd rather.'

'No, if you want to go home, that's what we'll do. As long as your parents don't mind.'

She kissed him. 'Thank you, Zachary. As for my parents, they love you too.' She leapt out of bed, 'I must go and tell Sam.'

They were ready to go in two days. Zachary was still very weak, but he insisted. When they stepped out on to the sidewalk. the street was full of people. The Lee brothers loaded their belongings on to a wagon to go to the depot.

Moose came forward rather tentatively and offered his hand. 'Thanks for all the help, Moose.' Zachary said to him.

'We'll probably see you in the spring,' Moose told them. 'This is my last boom town. I'd like to have a farm and a nice house for Ma and the girls. You wouldn't mind, would you?'

'No, we wouldn't mind,' Zachary told him.

Max and Jenny were there to say goodbye; it was their last boom town and they were coming to Montana, too. They'd buy some land, build a house, hire a cook and stay in bed for a year.

'Sounds nice,' Zachary told them.

Zachary shook hands with the Lee brothers. 'You coming to Montana, as well?' he asked.

'How would you manage without us?' Laredo asked.

The last person to come forward was Lester, accompanied by Mrs Sunstrom, Moose's mother. 'You want to come to Montana?' Zachary asked. 'We'll build you your own school.'

Tears welled in Lester's eyes, 'Do you want me to?' he asked.

Zachary considered the question. 'Well, not really,' he replied, 'but you still owe me two hundred thousand dollars.'

Lester wiped his eyes with his hand. He looked from Zachary to Mrs Sunstrom. She kissed him on the cheek. 'You go ahead, Lester, We'll see you in the spring.'

Lester disappeared for a few minutes then returned with his bag. 'I packed, just in case,' he said.

The crowd followed them to the depot. They put the luggage on board the train and put Buck in a wagon. So, it was time to go. Again there was much hand shaking and kissing. It seemed to Zachary that Lester and Mrs Sunstrom were very friendly.

'One last thing,' Zachary said. 'If you're coming to Montana, bring plenty of long johns, it's the coldest place on earth.' Clare hit him lightly, before helping him into the carriage.

They arrived back on Top Hat on the night that Clare's parents were having their Christmas

party for the hands and friends. The travelling
had taken its toll on Zachary and he felt weak.
They let themselves into the house and stood in
the doorway to the parlour. The house was
suddenly quiet. Steven and Margaret English
turned from talking to some of their friends, and
saw Zachary and Clare standing there. Zachary
looked very tired and was leaning heavily on
Clare. Margaret just stood and cried, looking at
her wonderful daughter and this strange, sad
man she had married.

'We're home, Zachary,' Clare said.

He squeezed her tight. 'Yes we are, Clare, yes,
we are.'